Home for the Holidays

A Holinight Novella

Lee Jacquot

HOME FOR THE HOLIDAYS

LEE JACQUOT

Cover Design: TRCDesigns

Edits: Nice Girl Naughty Edits

A Quick Note From the Author

Home for the Holidays is a standalone novella in the Holinights series. None of these books need to be read in order.

It is a steamy, filthy, and fun read where you'll need to suspend a little belief and just enjoy the ride. It is intended for mature audiences of legal adulthood age as it includes explicit consensual sexual scenes. It should NOT be used as a guide for kinks or a BDSM relationship.

The author is not liable for any attachments formed to the MCs nor the sudden desire to have someone wake you up with their tongue in your vag. ;)

Reader discretion is advised.

To the dreamers.

CHAPTER ONE

One degree colder, and I think my nipples will literally flash freeze, and break off.

It doesn't matter how long I've lived in Minnesota, I have never been able to get used to the shrill wind and temperatures that are so low, I sometimes entertain the thought of starvation in lieu of facing the elements and going to the store. Thank the big guy above for food delivery services. From pizza to the damn limes I always seem to forget when making cilantro rice, I don't ever have to leave the sweet, safe, *warm* confines of my home.

It's too bad I can't use them now to deliver me from the nightmare ahead.

"Did you find it?" My mother's voice is almost lost to the onslaught of wind that's been slapping against my face since I gathered enough moxie to open my car door.

My teeth involuntarily chatter as I stand upright, pulling the faux rock from the cluster of real ones near her peonies at the front porch, which are somehow thriving. They mock me with their vibrant colors, meanwhile, I'm the same hue as the snow that looks seconds away from breaking free from the low-hanging clouds. "Yep. Give me a sec."

Lifting my shoulder to pin the phone against my ear, I

fumble with gloved hands to slide the bottom plate of the rock open to reveal the spare key to my mother's house. It takes two ridiculous attempts of trying to squeeze my fingers inside the small opening before I mentally face-palm myself and tip it over in my hand.

I blame the cold. I'm pretty sure it damages brain cells.

I'm quick about shoving the key in the lock and pushing inside, nearly tripping on the way, courtesy of the next large gust. After I've managed to close the door, I grip the phone and grunt through clenched teeth. "I'm in."

"Twenty-six years here, and you still can't function in weather below thirty. I'm surprised you haven't up and left for Arizona by now."

I roll my eyes and grunt again. She knows exactly why I haven't given up the yards of snow and found sanctuary on a hot bed of sand somewhere. I'm her only family. Her only friend. It's especially true now since she and my stepdad of the past almost decade are days away from finalizing their divorce.

Todd is—*was*—a great husband. He was polite, helped around the house without being asked, gave Mom nightly foot massages after her twelve-hour shifts, and updated her on my volleyball games he never missed. They didn't argue, kissed way too much, and were both incredibly supportive in regard to anything that dealt with me or my stepbrother.

But even all that wasn't enough when it came down to it.

My mom has worked in the medical field since she graduated college and has always, *always*, put her career first. Over the years, as she grew as a surgeon, her schedule constantly changed, which sometimes meant missed birthdays and parent-teacher conferences. Dinner left in the fridge, and unsigned field trip forms.

I don't think it ever really bothered me because when we did spend time together, it was as though I was her whole world, and nothing else mattered. Not in those moments, at least. So when she did miss one of my games, or wasn't able to come to muffins-with-moms, I didn't mind because I knew she was saving someone's life.

Todd understood, too. Until he didn't.

Time off felt less substantial because as she aged, she needed more rest to recuperate between shifts, leaving the quality moments between them few and far between. Then, there was her refusal to retire anytime soon, severely affecting his plans to travel and see the world before sixty.

He felt guilty for wanting her to leave the profession, and she felt the same for not being able to commit time to their marriage. So, after eight years, they've decided to amicably split.

But not before one last Thanksgiving as a family.

Releasing a dramatic huff, I drop the grocery bags my driver, Winston, delivered to my place thirty minutes prior on the kitchen counter and slip into a barstool. The warm amber and cinnamon musk of the house settles into my lungs, melting my tight muscles.

The annoyance from the weather dissipates as my eyes trail over the familiar fall decorations my mother puts up every season. Be it the nostalgia or the realization that things are about to change, I manage to bite back whatever comment I consider making and smile into the receiver. "And leave you to figure out how to close the seventy-six open apps running in the background on your phone alone? You think so little of me, mother."

She laughs, and I imagine her shaking her head, the short midnight strands catching on the clasp of her glasses. "I'll have you know Cindy, in pediatrics, helped me delete all those applications I didn't need."

Chapter 1

Yes, the ones she was opening by accident but didn't let *me* delete because "she might want them later."

I can't stop my eyes from rolling, but manage to mask it in my voice. "How long will you and Todd be? Did you need me to start some stuff?"

It's still pretty early, but the quicker I begin, the quicker this can be over, and I can get back home where I don't have to socialize with anyone but Ryan Gosling on TV and a glass of Moscato.

Don't get me wrong, it's not as though I don't like Todd—it's the exact opposite—and knowing this is the last time I'll see them together is a little bittersweet.

They were married the summer before my senior year of high school, and even though I dreaded and severely opposed their union in the beginning, the joy he brought her was more than enough to make me rethink my position. And while their divorce is amicable, I know deep down, she's going to lose a bit of that joy.

"Actually, it may be a little longer than I thought. The ham is already done, but if you would go ahead and put it in the oven and then start the potatoes, that'd be great."

My eyes flit to the window above the sink. Just above the high peak of my old treehouse is a thick blanket of gray. It's a bit darker than it was this morning. "Be safe, and get here before it starts coming down."

"We will. Your brother will be there soon, and he's—"

My internal organs twist and turn so abruptly I can't even make out the rest of her sentence.

I hate when she calls him that.

Absolutely loathe it.

Elliot Rivera is not, or has never been, my *brother*.

A chill runs down my covered arms despite the warmth of the house and the bulk of my sweater. Memories of a time long before he was related to me try to shove to the forefront of my mind. A time of science projects and missed opportunities. Of gazes that lingered a second longer than they should and goosebumps that appeared anytime we were in the same vicinity.

Elliot Rivera is—was—many things, but I have never considered him a sibling.

Clearing my throat, I force myself to focus on what she's saying.

"You know he likes to taste test everything, so make sure he doesn't eat everything while it's still cooking."

"Sure. Will do." I push to my feet, and tug a loose strand of hair sticking out from under my beanie. "But I–uh, didn't know he was coming."

"Don't start, Todd. You said we could have the pumpkin pie. Yes, honey, of course, he's coming. It's our last holiday together."

A strange mix of unidentifiable emotions tightens around my throat.

Elliot hasn't made it to the past few Thanksgiving dinners, and before that, I was off at college halfway across the US, and couldn't come back.

How has it already been that long since we've been in the same room?

It's probably childish that I still even feel...nervous, when I think of him. Or perhaps it's trepidation. No. Maybe excitement. A little longing?

Admitting that, even in the safe confines of my own mind, seems wrong. Like when our parents exchanged *I do's*—even though we were months away from turning eighteen—it created a deep crevice in the sand. One that was vast and ever-expanding. Completely uncrossable, no matter how badly I wanted to risk it and jump across to the other side.

A heaviness weighs on my chest as I shoulder-shake off my

jacket and drop it on the chair I was just occupying. "Alright. I'll keep him from eating the food and get started on the ham and potatoes. Let me know when you're on your way, and I'll start the green beans."

"Thank you, honey."

We exchange goodbyes, and I quickly open up my music app in hopes of filling my mind with things other than Elliot. It's bad enough that I'll be seeing him face to face for the first time since graduation, I don't need to work myself up with overthinking how our reunion will go.

I'm sure if he's the same Elliot I remember during that year we were forced to live under the same roof, he'll say "hey" and act as though he can't see me squirming in my own skin.

I flip through my playlists till I find one that's supposed to get me motivated to hit the gym, but instead only ends up inspiring me to deep clean my entire apartment. The upbeat melody fills the kitchen as I set my phone down on the counter and strip off my hat, and kick off my boots.

It only takes a few minutes to unpack the groceries I brought and get the other food started before I realize I've forgotten about an old crush-turned-brother, and start wondering what life will be like without my stepdad, Todd, warming the recliner in front of the fireplace. It was one of the few things he'd brought over when they moved in, and if I remember correctly, it was a non-negotiable.

It'd been so funny watching my mom try to hold in the grimace tugging at her features.

Our quaint, two-story home is in a neighborhood built on the natural slope of a hill. Its face is covered in warm brown bricks with matching siding and black framed windows. Long curtainless windows line the front, the paved drive is natural cobblestone, and the garage is constructed from dark wood slates and illuminated by soft yellow lights. It's modern and sleek, as is the inside.

Todd's chair is mountain man meets mechanic and is the complete opposite of the chic modern decor my mom worked hard to create. The chairs' worn brown leather has long been buffed away to show the tan underside. Various small rips and cuts decorate a good twenty percent, but most are covered by an equally well-loved checkered blanket.

There wasn't a day that went by that he wouldn't sit in it while yelling at a football game with Elliot or watching a baking competition with me. He also sat there and went over college applications with us and helped me work on my scholarship stuff I didn't understand at the time. It's crazy how, in just a year's time, it'd become such a staple in my life during high school.

I'll miss that chair, but more importantly, I'll miss what it represents.

Overwhelmed with a sudden urge to sit in it one last time, I spare a quick glance over the food to make sure everything is fine before walking around the counter and into the living room.

My fingers graze smoothly over the top of the back before catching once on a torn piece of fabric as I move to the front. I sink down into the well-loved seat, and can't help the small smile tugging at my lips.

There was only one other time I dared to sit in this chair.

It was on one of the few occasions he and my mom went out for a date. I'd accidentally fallen asleep to Twilight.

I remember it through a bit of a sleepy haze, so the details aren't the clearest, but something distinct I won't ever forget was the fingertips and soft chuckle of my stepbrother.

The warm caress of his lip on the shell of my ear.

The tingle that radiated through my entire body as I waited

with bated breath to see what he would do. What he'd *finally* do.

But he didn't. I woke up the next morning in my bed, with nothing but a mild headache and faint recollection of *wanting* Elliot to finally push past the red tape.

After forcing out a weary breath, I grab either side of the chair to hoist myself up but stop short at the reflection of a figure in the fireplace's glass cover.

"Old habits die hard, don't they, sweetheart?"

CHAPTER TWO

Heart thrumming so hard I think it might fracture a rib, I jerk upright and turn to look at the owner of the voice.

With leather-bound arms folded across his chest, Elliot stands in all his bad-guy glory a yard away from me. Even almost a decade later, he doesn't look much different than senior year. Aside from the scruff on his tan face that's an hour past a five o'clock shadow, and the faint silver scar running along his right temple, he's still as gorgeous as I remember.

Standing just under six and a half feet tall, his lean, muscular shape has remained intact, complementing his strong jaw and deadly stare.

I remember when I first saw him freshman year of high school. He was the only person in the entire place who could somehow make the khaki slacks and white button-down look like the outfit to a mob intern. Rolled up sleeves, top button on his shirt undone, and tailored slacks, I pegged him for the trouble he radiated, and vowed to stay away.

But like any dangerous creature, he came with a veil of mystery that made even the most saintly at the academy want to taste the forbidden fruit.

Who knew how forbidden he would actually become just three short years later.

Deciding it's too late to act as if my mouth isn't open in half shock, half admiration, I simply close it and stand, lifting a hand in an awkward wave. "Hey."

Naturally, my voice comes out squeaky and annoyingly faint, but having not seen the man I once wanted with every fiber of my being, it's expected.

We keep up with one another in the family group chat, of course, but there, it's much easier to pretend he's not...well, *him*.

Elliot tilts his head, a barely-there gleam of amusement passing through his murky hazel eyes. A small flutter tickles my stomach as his gaze drops from my face to the chair, lingering for a moment too long. His eyes narrow, darkening for a hint of a moment as if he's recalling the same memory I was.

As expected, though, he corrects his features to his classic nonchalance and nods to the kitchen. "Where is everyone?"

I swallow thickly, walking from behind the chair and maneuvering carefully past him back into the kitchen. My pulse isn't beating any less quickly, and if I don't make myself busy, I'm bound to embarrass myself with more non-intentional ogling. "Still at the store picking some things up last minute."

"I'm surprised there are places open."

"Only one. Kowalski's. And she said they're only open for a few hours this morning."

Elliot's silence successfully tempts me to glance over my shoulder. His eyebrows are cinched together as if he's confused. After another beat, though, he must come to some sort of conclusion because he smirks to himself as he shucks off his jacket.

Of course.

Beneath the thick black fabric, a burgundy long-sleeve

thermal sticks to his chest and arms like a second skin. He's not bulky by any means, but the strength in his defined muscles is enough to make me wonder...to make me remember.

"So, how have things been going? You've been pretty quiet in the group text lately." Elliot rounds the counter and saddles up next to me at the sink. He pulls out a stalk of corn and strips it of its husks. "Anything interesting keeping you busy?"

My responding dry chuckle echoes in the small space around us. "If hibernating on the couch since the degrees drop below forty is interesting, then yeah."

Working as an at-home accountant for the investors of the world is both convenient and boring. The first two years, I devoted so much time to trying to learn the ever-changing market, I could barely take a second to breathe. But soon, I realized there was a pattern to their spending, and after a few months of switching my tactics to study the investors themselves, a lot of my job became use, rinse, and repeat. Because of that, in the winter at least, I'm able to devote my time to cozy gaming and binge-watching series I skipped out on during the nice summer months.

Elliot shakes his head. "I still don't get why you haven't moved yet. You work remotely, so you can go wherever you want."

I laugh, though it's humorless, and state what I feel is obvious. "My mom would be alone."

Elliot's lips draw down in the corners. "She works a lot. Not to mention, up until a few months ago, she had my dad to keep her busy. So what's the other reason?"

Partially annoyed that this is the direction of our first conversation, I scoff. "Well, the other seven months, I do love the weather."

"So you're content settling for only enjoying something half the time."

My brows draw up. Okay, this is definitely not how I thought this was going to go. "Bold assumption."

"Bold statement," he counters.

My molars smash together, an emotion I can't quite pinpoint pressing down on my chest.

I'm not a combative person. In fact, some would say I'm the easiest human in the world to get along with. I've always done what I'm told, followed the rules, and went above and beyond in any way I could. I partially blame the fact I had to grow up a little quicker than my peers since my mom was gone with work, but it allowed me to develop a solid discipline early in life, as well as teach me priorities and time management.

I didn't have time to mess around and fall behind in school. I couldn't risk the parties because half of them got broken up by police and sometimes got girls kicked off the volleyball team—a sport that I joined in hopes I could use it to get a scholarship so my mom wouldn't have to stress about college costs. I couldn't go to school dances because I was taking advanced courses, two of which counted as college credits, and the workload kept me busy. And I damn sure couldn't date because dating in our private school meant drama, and I had literally zero mental capacity for that.

Because of all of that, though, I kind of became a wallflower of sorts. Meek and quiet, only saying what was necessary so I didn't come off like a total bitch, but never enough to make too many friends. It's not as though I had time for those, either.

Now, all this goes without saying, it's not as if I didn't muse with the idea of what a normal teenage life would be like. What could be if I made one different decision? One small alternate choice.

Like right now, if I gave in to the tickle on my tongue and told my soon-to-be ex-stepbrother, he can shove it because he knows absolutely nothing about me. If I told him I've chosen not to move because of the same reasons I stayed to myself in high school. For the same reasons I chose solitude on my couch playing a farming simulation game instead of going to the bar with friends and having a mind-bending one-night stand.

I want to say it. I want to be honest. For once, I want someone to know that maybe, just maybe, I wish I didn't have to play it so safe in fear of getting hur—

As quickly as the spiral of thoughts began, I quickly shove them away. Maybe my mind is a little frazzled because of the dreaded weather, having to be alone with Elliot for the first time in forever, or because Mom is about to get a divorce.

Yeah, that's it. I just need a warm cup of tea—or wine—and probably a nap to set everything right.

Clearing my throat, I shake my head. "I love this state. It's beautiful."

Elliot nods slowly. "Says the person who hibernates."

"In the summer, I make it a point to do some hiking."

He hums, cleaning up the husks from the counter before washing the freshly skinned corn. It takes an embarrassing two minutes before a memory hits me. But that was so long ago. There's no way he remembers.

My gaze cuts toward him. "I thought it'd be fairly clear considering when I left for college in Florida, I never once said anything nice about it."

"You never said anything bad."

True. But before that, back when...I stop my train of thought again. Maybe I need something stronger than wine.

"Anyways. How have you been? I saw you fixed up that fifty-seven Aston Martin. It was gorgeous."

A shimmer of pride passes over Elliot's eyes. I've always thought they were magical, especially when he gives his rare smile. His iries's color is like the part of the ocean where two

13

currents meet. The deep blue crashing into the vibrant green, mixing in an angry, yet stunning collision.

My heart catches, heat engulfing my cheeks. I have to force my attention back to the potatoes, so I don't acknowledge that even after all this time, I'm still physically affected by my stepbrother.

It's supposed to feel naughty—gross, even. But the flip in my stomach is anything but.

Get a grip.

"It was. I hated that I only had it for one week." His lips thin into his normal half-grimace. I see that hasn't changed.

I'm not sure if I find solace in that or a little sadness.

"Anything exciting coming up?" I ask, fishing out the soft spuds and plopping them into a strainer.

Even in school, it was obvious where Elliot's path would take him. He was obsessed with cars, and not just your run-of-the-mill Chevy, or fast and furious brand-new Ferrari. He liked the classics. The *expensive* classics. So naturally, it came to no one's surprise when he started fixing and rebuilding them for collectors.

Elliot shrugs, taking a deep breath. "A few. But there's a different project I'm almost done with that I'm more focused on."

He glances at me in his periphery, an unreadable expression tightening his features.

"So." I chuckle awkwardly, grabbing the first potato to slice. "Don't keep me in suspense."

His eyes flash to the window and toward the treehouse briefly, but the shrill sound of his phone causes his parted lips to seal, whatever he was about to say swallowed up with it.

He dries his hand on the nearby embroidered turkey towel and slips out his cell. "Hey, Dad."

After listening for a moment, he nods. "Got it. It hasn't started here, so maybe you'll hit clear roads in a few miles."

He's quiet again. "Don't worry about it either way. We can always save it for later."

Elliot turns slightly, and I instinctively lean forward. It isn't until a sharp prick radiates across my hand that I realize I've cut the edge of my index finger. "*Shit.*"

I drop the knife and scoot over to the sink as Elliot whirls back around. He's confused for a moment until he looks down and shakes his head. "Be safe, Dad. Text me and let me know."

He quickly disconnects the call and grabs my wrist, wrapping his fingers around the flesh. The jolt of contact sends a slew of goosebumps prickling up my arm, and I try to pull away.

"I'm okay, I got it." I half-heartedly resist his hold, but he doesn't lessen his grip.

His lips pull down. "Says the person who almost cut her finger off right before a snowstorm."

A snow— "Oh no, are they okay?"

Elliot glides my hand under the lukewarm water and begins to wash the small wound. I jerk slightly at both the water and him. It's weird having someone take care of me in this way, washing a tiny cut I'm more than capable of dealing with myself.

"Yeah, just driving slowly through it. If it gets too bad, they may have to pull over and get a lodge."

My lips form a small o. Somewhere inside me, I know I should be disappointed we may not have been able to have the last dinner my mother really wanted, but instead, my entire nervous system is going haywire.

In no world would a night alone with Elliot be a good idea. *Shit.*

Chapter 2

If I didn't think I had a grip earlier, my hands are covered in slick oil now.

"You know what this reminds me of?" Elliot's voice snaps my attention to him. He's staring intently down at the cut, careful as he dries it. "That time in the treehouse when you got that splinter, and it took forever before you finally let me help. It was like it was the first time you ever let anyone help you with anything."

My face heats, and I turn my head toward the window. My eyes flit to the treehouse again, and this time, I can't stop the truth. Just this once, I'll make a different choice.

The choice to be a little vulnerable.

"It was."

CHAPTER THREE

EIGHT YEARS AGO

I rock on my heels, focusing on the burn in my calves instead of the myriad of nervous emotions bubbling in my chest.

Elliot Rivera has just pulled up to my house, and in some universe, I'm supposed to act like this is a normal Thursday night. Like it's every day that a hot, detached, suspected delinquent makes the active choice to have anything to do with me. Me. The head-down, straight-A girl, who would literally rather swallow a tablespoon of wasabi than congregate with anyone.

It's funny in the way one of those high school rom-coms would be, but depressing because it's real life. Elliot isn't Danny, and I'm surely not Sandy. There will be no riding off in the clouds in his greased Ford. Instead, I'm pretty sure I'm going to overthink this entire next couple hours till I'm old and gray, always wincing when recalling whatever completely idiotic thing I'm bound to say.

Elliot and I are part of a five-person group in our junior biology class, and today was the only option that fit into all of our schedules to meet and work together. Ten minutes ago, though, Linda texted that she had an emergency cheer session.

Timothy called because his mom needed him to do a shift at her restaurant because of a no-show. And Jim, well, he's Jim, so I don't believe anyone really expected him to come, but still. Without them, I won't have any buffers between Elliot and me.

I've always and inexplicably been a wreck around him, and without anyone to help distract me from all that is him, I'm not sure how I'll make it without fumbling over my words at some point, or just making a fool of myself in general.

"So... *everyone* bailed," I announce to Elliot as he exits his car, his gaze doing a quick sweep of my frame, then the house behind me.

Tensing slightly as if he's doing a three-second evaluation of my entire life and value, I hold my breath. I'll admit it's a tad ridiculous to let another person choke me up this much, but it does make me feel better that eighty-nine percent of the school's populace does the same thing when he's around.

Elliot grunts, though whether it's at me, my house, or that no one else is coming is unknown. He locks his car, his features unchanging from his cemented, bored expression. He's always so indifferent, never visibly bothered by anything going on around him—even when it actively affects him.

I both hate and admire that quality. It must be nice not to have people so easily read you, but also, it's terrible for the rest of us who aren't able to gauge anything about him.

Turning to lead him up the cobblestone path that leads to the front door, I motion to the shiny car he pulled up in. "Is that a classic?"

I'm not inept, but I don't know anything about cars. I don't know what's considered foreign or antique, or how to even begin to identify a collectors' edition or a year when the best automobiles were made. But in no way do I regret asking what felt like a ridiculous question, because when his deep hazel eyes flicker to me, I could swear amusement flashes through them.

It's gone before I can be sure. "It's a sixty-seven Impala. It was my dad's in high school."

"Impressive that it still runs." Another absurd statement, but I'm rewarded with his lips twitching in what I believe is a smirk.

My stomach flips over on itself as I delight in the tiny inkling of a breakthrough. Elliot and I have been in school together since freshman year, been in six various classes together, and never have I seen him smile.

"With proper maintenance, I'm pretty confident it will last longer than that."

He nods to Mom's electric Fiat. A gift from my dad before he decided he liked his other family in Naples a lot more. I nod, my lips thinning. "You're probably right. Yours would be a better choice in the zombie apocalypse, too, I'm sure."

A sound eerily similar to huffed, dry laughter scatters in the air behind me. "No. It would be too loud."

I'm so tempted to turn around, but I know the second I do, my downward spiral will ensue. Instead, I release a goofy, short burst of a noise that's supposed to be a giggle. "True. And if they're anything like WWZ, you'd be done for."

I expect that to be the end of the conversation, for us to move silently inside and for me to spend the next twenty minutes trying to broach the silence and get something—anything—out of the stone wall. But then Elliot surprises me.

He steps in front of me and grips the black iron door knob of my front door to open it for me. "Absolutely. I need them to be like Shaun's. Slow, a little dull."

I'm pretty positive I say something, but I'll never know for sure. The little synapses in my head are sparking so rapidly from the close proximity to him, I can't function. He's a foot away, but his warm, earthy scent wafts over me, and I'm finally able to see just how much I haven't been able to appreciate.

Now I can make out that his top lip is a hint bigger than his bottom. His jaw has lost the roundness of youth and is starting to sharpen, while his other features are becoming more strong. And his eyes. His *eyes*. Words have all but escaped me when I look at the various shades of green and blue fighting a war in his irises.

Even in my own head, I can hear how obsessed I sound. How completely enthralled I am with a boy I don't know much about. But right now, at this moment, when he's this close, and we're having a conversation about which zombies we want to endure at the end of days, I can't help but not care.

"I agree. They wouldn't last longer than a week in the snow we get."

Oh. I said something about our weather. Heat blooming on my cheeks, I laugh. This one is much less deranged. "Very true. Ten inches, and they wouldn't move. But also, if they froze, would they be able to—"

"Thaw out and continue living in the spring?" Elliot nods as though in deep thought over it and pulls my door open. "It makes sense."

Unable to hide the stupid smile from stretching across my face, I hurry inside, butterflies whipping violently in my stomach.

"Beautiful house," Elliot says from behind me. "I always wondered what the houses up here looked like inside."

I release a soft sigh. "Thank you. It was one of my dad's designs. This whole neighborhood was actually."

The silence I'm met with causes me to peek at him over my shoulder. His hands are shoved in the front of his black jeans, his shoulders hitched up a fraction. If it weren't for the completely indifferent mask of his features, I would guess he felt something.

After another beat, I gesture to the kitchen just past the foyer. "We can set up at the island, or at the table. There should be enough space."

He gives me a curt nod. "Whatever you want."

Whatever I want.

Images of his lips on mine hit me before I can stop them, and within a second, I already know my face is engulfed in a shade of crimson.

Clearing my throat, I whip my head back around and walk a bee-line to the island where I initially set everything up. It's better to sit beside him than across, that way I'm not forced to look him in the face every time I glance up. At least, that's what I tell myself when I start to explain what all we need to get done.

He listens to me rattle off the list, his eyes glossing over the materials on the counter, and when I'm done, he immediately gets started.

Thirty minutes pass, and while my face has likely lessened in its extreme blush thanks to my Adam's Family comparable shade, the heat hasn't. Every time I turn to grab a paper, it never fails that our hands brush against one another. When he prints something from the copier and passes behind me, his hips narrowly clip mine. And when I'm sketching out on the poster, I can feel the blaze of his stare on every part of me.

Could this all be wishful thinking in my head? Yeah, definitely, but when I purposely drop my pencil to test the theory, my thoughts are validated.

He bends at the same time I do, and when our fingers collide over the writing utensil, theoretical and physical sparks fly. A static shock snaps us both, but instead of jerking his hand back like I do, his heavy gaze settles on mine, and his lips part.

21

We're frozen in time and in place, both of us now inches apart. My breath quickens, and despite his unreadable expression, I see it. The attraction? The curiosity? I don't know. I'm not sure, but I can almost bet he's about to kiss me, and I'm going to let him.

Holy crap, Elliot Rivera is about to kiss me.

"I promise that you'll never find another like me!" Both my mother and Taylor suddenly blaring from a speaker, sing in unison, shattering the bubble he and I were surrounded by.

My eyes seal shut as I stand, the upbeat music echoing from the master bedroom and through the rest of the house. "Sorry. My mom is getting ready for a date. I'll go tell her to turn it off."

Elliot slowly rises and shakes his head. "That's okay. I actually think it's time for a break anyway."

My brows cinch together in part annoyance at my mom for ruining our moment and the other in worry. He's probably going to say it's a break and go drive to get something and never come back. Probably both realizing he was about to make a huge mistake, and also deciding this school project is too big for two people.

I clear my throat. "Yeah, sure. Of course. I'll keep going over the—"

"Would you mind showing me what *that* is?"

My gaze flickers to his, and I follow his line of sight out of the kitchen window leading to my tree house. It's pretty big, whereas treehouses go, resting about twelve feet in the air and housing two hundred square feet. There was a time I tried to make it my bedroom, but quickly realized without a bathroom, it wasn't really sustainable.

Still, if Mom isn't home, I stay in it until sundown.

"Sure."

He follows me out of the kitchen and toward my sanctuary. Its sides and front are covered in wood that's a light oak color, but the back—my favorite part—is a giant glass window.

When we climb up the narrow set of stairs, my pulse begins thrumming hard again, but I desperately try to focus on each step so I don't fall. Inside there is a couch, a desk, an art station, bookshelves, and a huge bean bag. If my dad had still been here after he got it done, I'd have electricity too, but for now, solar lights it is.

Elliot is silent as he looks around, his fingers unabashedly grazing over my shelves and the titles of some of the books nestled on them. My heart falters as he examines the space, his feet finally coming to a stop when he reaches the window.

With his back to me, I wait. My mind racing, not being able to reign in my array of emotions or settle on one singular thought. When he finally speaks, the air grows thin.

"This is the first place I'd come whether there were the slow or rabid zombies."

A smile cuts across my face, and the ache in my cheeks is instant. "It's my favorite place in the world."

He nods, turning around. "It's easy to see why."

I bite into my lip, hoping it will stop the dozens of things I want to say from spilling out. Like how when it rains, I could come up here and draw an entire galaxy on two sheets of paper. Or when it's snowing, the amazing insulation is thick enough that I sit up here for hours reading until the little solar lights finally stutter off.

How on the clearest summer night, I fall into my bean bag and make a wish on every last star.

"Can I tell you something, Adelina?"

"Yes." My voice is nothing but a whisper.

He takes a slow, deliberate step toward me, and I suck in a sharp breath.

Elliot pauses, a genuine smirk curling the ends of his lips.

For a moment, when those lips part I wonder if he's about to tell me a lifelong secret of how he's been head over heels in love with me and waited all this time before confessing. Or maybe that he just realized how he has a thing for the quiet, hard-working types.

But instead of either, or something even remotely in the same realm, he grips the nape of his neck and sighs. "I'm having a hard time understanding the unit. The chemistry of it is diffi-cult for me."

My heart squeezes painfully in my chest, and a heaviness I can't possibly understand settles on my shoulders with the real-ization that I am a stupid, foolish girl.

I blink at least three times as I back away and walk to my desk. "Oh, got you. Um, sometimes it's easier to show it as a visual. Let's try that."

Small little tremors shake my hands as I try to find my chalk, but after a moment, I become overly frustrated at both my wishfulness, and the stark reality, so I grab my Sharpies.

Elliot sits on the couch as I take the markers over to a blank wall. Without thinking, I lose myself in something I know. Something I can distract myself with while I attempt to get my silly little heart rate under control. I'm scribbling so quickly, and explaining so much that soon, the air isn't as thick, and the room opens back up.

When I'm done, I glance back at Elliot as a fellow group member and not as the guy I wish would see me and not the wall I so clearly blend into.

He asks a few questions, and on the last one, when I point, a sharp prick digs into my finger. "*Ouch.*"

Elliot stands and is next to me before I've even made out what it was that stabbed me. "Are you okay?"

I nod, trying to ignore his closeness. "Yeah, just a splinter."

He holds his hand out. "Let me see."

"It's fine."

He shakes his hand impatiently. "Adelina, let me help you. You got it because of me."

Narrowing my eyes, I spot the small piece of wood invading the delicate flesh of my fingertip. He lets me attempt an extraction twice before he releases an exasperated breath. "Let. Me. See."

"*I got it.*" my words come out a little snippier than necessary, and I immediately look up to apologize. "Sorry, it's just...okay."

Reluctantly, I place my hand in his. The warmth of his skin heats my entire body, the shock from earlier sparking the hopeful flame I just stamped out. My traitorous eyes examine his concentrated face, his furrowed brows, and the tightness in his jaw.

He may not want me, but it doesn't negate how utterly gorgeous he is.

My eyes close briefly at the thought, and when they open again, Elliot's gaze is on mine. It flits between me and my lips, and for two seconds, I ignore it. There's no point in getting hurt three times in a day. But the second he leans forward, I melt. The earlier thoughts and situations gone as he inches closer.

This is real. It's happening.

But it seems fate is much crueler than I once thought because the roar of an engine causes Elliot to snap upright. Without a word, he walks to the door of my treehouse, wrenching it open with a curse.

It takes an embarrassing few seconds before I'm able to follow behind him to see what's going on.

"How did I not put that together?" he mutters, and for the first time, Elliot's emotion is clear. He's angry. No, not angry. Livid.

From our vantage point in the tree, I can only make out a

little bit of the driveway and a car that's not too unlike Elliot's. "Who is that?"

His jaw stiffens. "My father."

I rear back slightly, confusion marring my features. "Your dad? But why is he..."

"He told me he has a date."

My heart plops into my stomach with a sickening thud as nothing else is said, and instead, we watch my mother loop her hand around his father's arm and saunter to the car.

We take a shuttered breath in unison.

It's fine. It's perfectly fine. My mom goes on a date at least once a month, and nothing usually pans out because she's just looking for a good time, and nothing more.

I'm sure this will be the same.

I mean, really, what's the worst thing that could happen?

CHAPTER FOUR

I 'll never forget the day my father asked me to help him
pick out a ring to marry Adelina's mother.

Adelina. The very same girl I'd been infatuated with
since I walked through the doors of Wilmith Academy and laid
eyes on her fighting to open her locker. She kept to herself,
studied hard, and was ignorantly unaware of how fucking
gorgeous she was.

I'm not a timid guy. If I ever wanted something, I got it. Be
it a materialistic thing, or the most sought-after girl in school.
But there was something about Adelina. It warned me I needed
to be patient. Take it slow. The only problem was the rest of the
school allowing me that time.

Despite her introverted demeanor, every fucking guy there
wanted her, all of them taking bets on who'd be able to break
through her high walls and get her. Idiots. She was mine even
before I even knew her last name, and I happily broke a few
noses to make it known.

Too bad in the end, it didn't matter anyway. Somehow, my
father ran into her mother when he was in surgery recovering
from a kidney stone that he couldn't pass. He did what he did
best, and the next thing I know, he was down on one knee—

27

making the little progress I'd made up until that moment useless.

My father had known I liked Adelina. Known how long I'd waited to make my move. But he said, being his age, love didn't come around as often as it would for me. I was just a kid. She wasn't the one. *I had time.*

Time. The same thing I'd had for the past three years as I'd slowly gotten closer to her. As I waited.

I was pissed, but knew trying to fight him on it would do nothing, so instead, I pleaded for him to wait. Just until after my senior year, so I wouldn't have to live with her. So I wouldn't have to be under the same roof and try not to look at my fucking step-sister like I didn't want to fuck her on every surface of that damn treehouse.

But that's exactly what I had to do. I had to see her every goddamn morning and night, make small talk in the hall, help clean our communal bathroom, look at her across the dinner table with nothing but a blank face, and not react when I passed her room at night and the door was open.

She liked to do that sometimes, usually when she was exhausted after one of her games, but I still wondered if it was somehow on purpose. If she enjoyed testing my self-restraint.

When she was sleeping, it never failed that she'd kick off the comforter. Her oversized shirt would always be lifted, exposing her curves, toned legs, and an ass I wanted to bury my cock in. I wanted every fucking part of her, and if there was the smallest hint that she didn't care that I was now legally her brother, I would have done it despite the aftermath. Would have stripped her down and devoured her sweet pussy before shoving my dick so far inside her she'd feel me there for weeks.

I wanted her to feel how long I'd waited for her.

How bad I fucking wanted her.

Somehow, though, none of that happened. I stayed in a

place more discouraging than the friendzone, and had to grin and fucking bear it.

Who knew having patience would pay off? That eight years later, my feelings would be the same.

With our parents' divorce, there's no longer an obstacle to overcome; no forbidden element blocking me from what I so desperately want. And this time, I'm not going to skirt around the obvious. She's mine now as much as she was eight years ago, and it's time she understood.

After drying Adelina's small wound, I lift her hand and incline it toward the bright overhead light. It's a little deeper than a paper cut, but it won't need much besides a bandaid.

Keeping her hand in mine, I walk us to the edge of the kitchen to a drawer where her mother keeps the first aid kit. I'm quick to open it up and dig inside for a waterproof bandage. Using my teeth, I rip off the top of the package, my gaze on Adelina.

Her lashes flutter.

Yeah. Still mine.

"I thought we'd stopped this habit of you accidentally hurting yourself around me," I tell her, securing the bandage around her finger.

During our depressingly long year living under the same roof, there was more than one occasion she tripped over her feet, hit the corner of walls with her shoulder, or slammed a hand in the cabinet.

"It's because you make me nervous." Her breath hitches as the confession escapes. Her realization she didn't mean to say that part out loud turning her cheeks a delicious pink.

I level her with an expressionless stare, my eyes lowering briefly to a mouth I've fantasized about more times than I'd like to admit. Adelina's chest begins to rise and fall faster, the quick thump of her pulse in her neck proving her words true. Still, I need to know the reasons.

"How do I make you nervous, sweetheart?"

Her lips part, the blush deepens, and my cock twitches. It grows harder the longer the silence stretches, and just when I'm sure she won't answer, she whispers, "Because I can't read you."

I draw back slightly, a little surprised. "You're nervous because you don't know what I'm thinking?"

She nods. It's slow and bashful, her dark eyes barely visible under her thick row of lashes. "It's similar to how people fear what they don't understand. I've never been able to figure you out."

I arch a brow. "You've tried?"

"Of course. Since I first met you," she scoffs. "And then when I became your siste—"

My grip around her hand tightens. "I have never seen you as my sister."

She swallows thickly. "I'm not sure if that's supposed to be an insult or..."

Adelina's voice trails off, and her eyes dip away. It isn't until this moment that I realize I hate when she's not looking at me. I'm annoyed even more that the action makes my sternum draw tight. I hook a finger under her chin and turn her face back toward me.

"If you want to know something." Lifting her injured hand, I press my lips softly over the bandage. "All you have to do is ask."

A long, weighted moment passes between us, an understanding settling thick in the air. I'm transported back to the day in the treehouse when I was seconds away from kissing her.

I want to kiss her now.

My gaze sinks to her lip she has tucked inside her teeth. I release her hand so I can tug the sensitive flesh free, but when I move, she takes it either as a sign, or misreads what I mean to do and steps back. She clears her throat and shakes her head as if that will somehow erase the words I've said. Erase the meaning.

"So, everyone bailed," she jokes. "Again."

A smirk lifts one corner of my mouth. "Looks like it. Still want to finish?"

Adelina glances around at the half-cooked food, likely having a similar thought process as myself. After a moment, she nods, her eyes returning to mine. "Might as well. Want to watch Christmas Vacation?"

It's an annual tradition I learned Adelina and her mom had when we moved in. Cook Thanksgiving dinner, watch the movie, then decorate for Christmas. Something strange lifts in my chest that she wants to continue the tradition without anyone else here.

"Yeah. Sounds good."

She beams, spinning on her heels to grab the remote from the living room. When she returns, there's something different about her. Something I can't put my finger on. "So since they aren't coming, we don't have to make pumpkin pie right?"

I shake my head. "Fuck, no."

She laughs and sound washes over me like a hot shower after being under the hood of a car all day. "Great."

I watch in a brief silence as she spins toward the counter and starts collecting supplies to make her apple pie cookies.

I'm not going to fuck it up this time. Tonight, Adelina will learn there hasn't been a day that's passed since our freshman year that she wasn't mine.

CHAPTER FIVE

T hankfully, Thanksgiving dinner has only ever consisted of just us four—not counting the times Elliot or I had an excuse for not coming—so there isn't an absurd amount of food to prepare.

Chevy Chase plays on the mounted TV in the living room as background noise while we spend the next hour cooking. Twice I call my mom to ensure her and Todd are fine. They checked into a local hotel, ordered two separate room services, and are arguing over what movie to fill the time with until the storm passes and they can try to get here.

I'm likely supposed to feel guilty when I told her on both calls that they should stick it out and wait till tomorrow, but I don't.

I don't feel guilty for enjoying the dozen times I've turned around and caught Elliot's eyes lingering on me. I don't feel guilty for allowing him to get closer than necessary when he grabs the utensils on my other side. And I must certainly don't feel guilty for considering what I would do if he tried to kiss me again.

My entire body engulfs in a forbidden heat when I picture those dangerous eyes playing with mine as he pressed his lips on my finger. How his pupils flared, and the corner of his lips twitched.

At that moment, for just two seconds, I didn't see my step-dad's son. I didn't see the detached and bored bad boy who always appeared to be waiting for nothing and everything all at once.

No. At that moment I saw just Elliot. The guy who fought me to take a splinter out of my finger, or once showed me that if I hit my locker twice near the bottom hinge, it would open. The guy who started a program in his automotive class during senior year that offered free minor repairs to anyone who received a ticket in the last thirty days.

I saw the guy I was infatuated with even before I knew much about him.

Or maybe I did. Maybe something inside of me saw the little, minuscule parts of him and began stockpiling it until I knew I'd fall for him if ever given the chance.

"What are you thinking about?" Elliot's voice acts as a loud clap, yanking me from my musing.

"Huh?" I force my breathing to even before glancing at him. His head is cocked to the side, a brow raised and two glasses lifted as though he's been waiting.

"What are you thinking about?" He repeats.

"Nothing." I lie, shrugging nonchalantly even though heat is creeping up my neck from his intense gaze.

"Really?"

"Yes."

He smirks, and my heart trips. "Then can I ask why you've been cutting that same piece of spinach for a good five minutes?"

My brows scrunch together before I realize my hand is, in fact, moving up and down in an animatronic motion. I let my gaze drop and sure enough, a poor, wilted clutter of spinach has been minced past recognition.

"Oh...I" I clear my throat before swiping the spinach into the sink. "I guess I was distracted."

Elliot huffs before shaking his head. "Come on. I'm tired of waiting."

My eyes flit to his in question, but he turns and walks to the dining room table without another word.

With a deep sigh, I tell myself five times that his odd phrasing wasn't odd at all, and I'm overanalyzing it because *I* am tired of waiting.

But for what? I don't know.

Chest tight, stomach empty, and heart pounding, I follow behind Elliot with two bowls of spinach-less salads.

Without our parents, one would imagine the room would feel empty, or that something significant was lacking, but with the electric air crackling around the table, and the weight sitting heavy between us, I can barely breathe. It's exciting and exhilarating, while also nerve-wracking and a little scary.

Is it possible I've read everything wrong? That I've over-played every moment that's slipped between us? Maybe?

I mean, he *is* still technically my step-brother. This would still be considered taboo if anything did happen. This—whatever this is—is still as forbidden today as it was eight years ago.

Do something drastic.

The thought careens into me out of nowhere and I immediately shove it away. I'm not impulsive. Everything I do has been thought through at least twenty times over, the pros and cons scaled and weighed before I take a single step. I can't just act and hope for the best. I should wait it out. Wait for a more direct sign.

But I want to know now.

My eyes drift across the hardwood table, over the servings

of mashed potatoes, green bean casserole, and sliced ham. Elliot's gaze is on me, a knife's tip twirling at the edge of his lip.

A foreign heat blazes through my body, cutting through my veins and incinerating my core. All of a sudden, my sweater is too thick, and pants too tight.

I try swallowing twice, and on the third, I have to grab a glass of water. How am I this ridiculous around him? It's not as though I haven't dated before. Haven't flirted with a man or picked up on tell-tale signals of interest.

But Elliot—so help me—has always been difficult for me to figure out. For me to understand.

Screw it. It's time to ask flat out, and if I'm embarrassed in the end, oh well. Our parents are divorcing so it's not as though I'll see him again.

That new thought gives me pause as an acute pain pinches something in my chest. After tonight, I would have no reason to ever see him again. No reason for us to be in the same room.

"Would you have ever done anything like that?" Again, Elliot pulls me from my thoughts.

I blink. "Done what?"

He nods to the TV before lowering the knife to his plate, his eyes still locked on me. "Flash people while on a road trip."

My brows tic together before I glance at the movie playing. It must have started after Christmas Vacation ended. It's currently on a scene where a family is on a road trip and the two teenage girls in the backseat flash any cars with older boys, unbeknownst to the parents driving.

I roll my eyes and quickly get up to grab the remote to change it. "No. Definitely not."

"Why not?"

The sincerity in his question makes me snort a bit of laughter. "What do you mean, why wouldn't I flash random guys on a road trip?"

He shrugs. "A show of youthful rebellion."

"I didn't have a reason to rebel." Not a lie. But also, not one hundred percent true either.

I completely and utterly support my mom as a general surgeon. I've heard her stories for as long as I can remember of the families she's healed, the people who no longer have chronic pain, and so on and so forth. But deep down, under everything, I missed her. A lot.

Did I hate that I had to grow up and do for myself ninety percent of the time? Yes. Did it bother me when she had to work, it felt as if I didn't exist? Sure. Somewhere inside was I angry I couldn't live the life of a normal teen? Maybe.

I had a great life—a great childhood—even though she wasn't around often. I was always provided for, well-fed and clothed, and never went without. So no, I never wanted to rebel. Well...not until him.

He was the polar opposite of me while the same in so many ways.

Both quiet, but while he worked on cars after school, I studied.

Both of us kept to ourselves, but while he found himself in fights at least once a month, I spoke to one other person besides my teacher.

Both single all four years of school, but girls did everything they could to get his attention, while not one guy looked my way.

I was interested because we were so similar, yet so different, and I was tempted to know how he saw the world.

But then, as soon as I thought I would get to learn, he was taken away by the one person who could.

Shaking my head, I use the remote to scroll until I get to *A Christmas Story*, and sit back down at the table. "No, but I may have had the occasional dream of less-than-perfect acts."

"Dreams." Elliot's head quirks to the side in interest. "Care to share?"

My heart thuds a little faster. It'd be so easy to say it right now. Tell him how many nights I fantasized about him. How many times I left my door open in case one night he decided he didn't care as much as I wish I didn't. That it wasn't just one dream, but dozens I wished were reality.

But as much as I crave I could part my lips to utter the words, I am who I am, even if annoyingly so. I don't take risks because I've never been granted the luxury. And honestly, I'd much rather live with Elliot always being a *what if* in my life, than a flat-out rejection. I don't believe my feelings could handle that, not with how deep and how long they've run.

Shaking my head, I divert my eyes and begin eating a slice of the ham. "Nothing too crazy."

"Hmm," he grunts, but I refuse to look at him only to be met with that same, almost disappointed glower on his face.

Instead, I continue focusing on the food in front of me for the next ten minutes, only glancing up to grab my water glass or watch small snippets of the movie. It isn't until I'm almost done eating that Elliot finally speaks.

"Do you ever wonder what would've happened if our parents didn't get married?"

A humorless, sad-tainted smile breaks across my face. "Back then, almost every day."

"Why?"

My mouth opens and closes before I sigh and glance up at him. His gaze is what I expected—bored, but intense—though a small tendon that pulses in this jaw tells another story. Something past the surface of what he's showing me.

Then it hits me like the kid in the movie who realized not to put his tongue on a frozen pole.

In high school, there were a few occasions I thought he was

flirty, when I could have sworn he was hitting on me. But I couldn't possibly fathom it being *me* he was choosing. Not when the girlfriend options were vast and many, and none of them were hermits. Today has followed that similar theme. Like he's casting out the fishing line and waiting for me to bite. It's as though he needs me to make the first move so he knows it's real.

We've both been waiting on the other. Too worried about the circumstances, our lives before, and our lives now to just out and do something.

We've been living the forbidden, miscommunication trope of life.

Goddamn it.

CHAPTER SIX

I swear if my revelation turns out to be a massive misread on my part, and I end up rejected, I will never crawl out of the hole of my condo ever again.

Pulse thrumming, and anxiety whipping through me so fast the air feels all but existent, I rush the words out. "Because I wanted you."

Elliot falls silent for a moment before his absurdly perfect lips slightly part, allowing his tongue enough room to sneak out and sweep along the edge. "You wanted me?"

A vengeful blush flares across my face and down the middle of my body, engulfing the raging butterflies in a blaze. But now that I've started, I force myself to continue. I can't chicken out this time. This is it.

"Yes, along with everyone else in our graduating class."

"Yet you never said anything." A statement, not a clarifying question.

I scoff, standing to gather my empty plate. "Elliot, you know me well enough to know I'm not the most talkative type, especially back then."

His mouth tugs down in the corners. "Neither am I."

True. But also, I'm not the one asking him why he didn't pursue me. I grab a few of the smaller, empty dishes and pile them together. "Does it matter, Elliot? Our parents ended up together anyway, so it would have been in vain in the end."

"Not really, considering they're divorced."

"About to be divorced," I correct him, walking into the kitchen. We cleaned up as we were cooking, putting extras in the Tupperware containers, meaning there isn't much to keep my hands busy as this conversation gears up to who knows what.

"Either way." Elliot appears, carrying his own set of dishes. "It would have been nice to know."

"Why?"

Elliot doesn't respond and after a few seconds of me cleaning up what little's left in the kitchen, I finally take the bait and turn around, propping my hands behind me on the counter, ready for whatever nonchalant comment he hits me with. But instead, I find him staring out of the kitchen window, toward the treehouse.

His profile is strong, his gaze thoughtful. Even under the gray overcast sky, which makes him look much more ominous and glum, he's still beautiful.

"Do you think it's still there?"

"Is what there?" I ask, confusion and curiosity prompting me to turn and peer out the window with him.

"The diagram you drew me that day."

Me, nor the goosebumps that instantly sprout along my arm, need him to elaborate on which day he's referring to. Pulse fluttering, I shake my head with a shrug. "It's been a while since I've been out there but I wouldn't assume either way. The insulation is great, and it's away from direct sun, so perhaps."

To be honest, I haven't been back in the treehouse since Todd proposed. I told myself it was because senior year kept me busier with college prep and graduation, but I'd be lying if I said I didn't want to be where Elliot was. I was curious about him before he moved in, it was only natural that curiosity peaked when we lived under the same roof.

Elliot takes a step back and extends a hand toward the back door. "Want to find out?"

My brows pull together. "You want me to go outside, in freezing weather with a storm moving this way, to see if a drawing is still on the wall?"

He grabs his jacket from the back of a barstool. "Yes, I want you to come outside with me, in freezing weather to see if it's still there."

I choke out a sarcastic laugh. "A storm is coming, Elliot. I'm not going out—"

"It went East."

"What?"

"The storm, sweetheart." Elliot grabs my jacket from the other stool and walks to me. My core tightens as he nears, his gaze reminding me of a predator's stare right before they dominate their prey. "It missed us."

"But I live to the East," I whisper as he wraps my bulky coat around my shoulders.

He smirks, something both mischievous and knowing in his eyes. "Guess you'll have to stay here tonight."

I don't find the words to respond to both that look or the fact I'll be staying the night in my childhood home, because Elliot grabs my hand and leads me out into the backyard.

The wind is softer than this morning, only whooshing by and not feeling like an all-out assault, but it's still too cold to willingly be out here. "Do you really need me to come?"

I give a longing glance back to the glowing house, before a sound I've never heard before echoes in the air around me.

My head whips toward Elliot whose expression has already changed back to a solemn frown, forcing me to wonder if I made up the faint laughter in my head. But when he glances at me from his periphery, a corner of his lip lifts. But whatever he considers saying, dies when we reach the stairs.

Even though they're narrow, he continues to hold my hand and tug me up after him, only releasing me when he reaches the small patio.

"Code still the same?" Elliot taps the small keypad we'd added after a raccoon learned how to turn the handle. A mess I still shudder to think about.

I nod, and watch him press the buttons in quick succession. I'm not sure if I can blame it on the cold when a shiver racks through me as he inputs the code he only ever saw me enter once, eight years ago.

The box turns green, beeping twice before the lock clicks into place. He opens the door, gesturing for me to enter first, before following close behind. Inside, it isn't much different from when I'd move some things out before graduation, which surprises me as by now, the whole thing should be coated in layers of dust. But no, the spines of the books that were left behind, are clear and legible. My art supplies are in the cups, organized and color-coded. Even the beanbag, couch, and small rug look as though they've been regularly fluffed and vacuumed.

It's not far-fetched to assume my mother is responsible. She's an empty nester and soon to be a second time divorcee. Perhaps this fills her time when she's off of work, keeps her mind busy.

A heaviness moves in my chest as I truly consider it. Here I am, a considerable mess, worrying about the whole will-he-won't-he with Elliot while my mom is dealing with much more. Not only that but she had to spend Thanksgiving with her ex in some hotel, ordering room service.

"What if they hook up tonight?" I say as suddenly as the idea blooms. "I mean, they're snowed in, at the end of their marriage. Isn't that when people start remembering the beginning of it all?"

Elliot huffs. "I'm not sure if you're being serious or projecting, but our parents have two very different visions of where they want their lives to go, so I can almost guarantee nothing is going to happen between them."

A line creases between my brows. "But you don't know for sure. Also, what do you mean, projecting?"

His eyes widen a fraction before he passes a hand between the two of us. "You're a smart woman, Adelina. I'm sure you know what I mean."

"While I appreciate the compliment, I would like to ask for a little clarification. I believe we keep misreading what the other is saying, and it's becoming a tad cumbersome."

He shakes his head, seemingly entertained he has to break such a trivial thing down further for me to understand. "Here we are, the last time we'll ever be required to be in the same room. You're snowed out of your home for the night, and I've brought you here to look at a drawing that could have been the start of us."

The air is suddenly much warmer, as is my body. We've yet to come right out and be honest with the truth lingering just out of reach, I'm scared to actually grasp it. Scared of what it will mean. We're still technically siblings after all.

As though he can read my thoughts, he takes a weighted step toward me, the same, dark intense stare from the kitchen back in place. It sends a shock of arousal into my blood, and I have to squeeze my fists together to keep my body from responding.

He stops less than a foot away, his chest so close it would brush against mine if he took a deep breath. His signature scent of clean musk, and a hint of something masculine washes over me, clinging to my skin like morning dew.

Hazel eyes rake over me slowly, but instead of it feeling as though he's evaluating every aspect for flaws, it's as if he's memorizing every corner of my face. It's....intimate.

I hold my breath, my heart pounding so hard that I can sense it in the tips of my toes. Everything around us is both unmoving and unsteady, and I'm unable to focus on anything else except him. How much I still want him, even after all this time.

When he's finally done with his slow perusal of me, he leans an inch closer, his head dipping down and angling toward my ear. "I can make it clearer if you'd like, sweetheart."

I swallow hard, grasping at any words that I might be able to string together and make a coherent sentence. "Maybe you should."

A demand said in a voice I barely recognize, but Elliot's response is worth every bit of courage it took.

He smirks, reaching up and hooking a finger beneath my chin to tip it up. "Do you see that drawing behind me?"

My eyes flit to the faded sharpie on the wall that barely shows the work of a mitochondria. Just recalling that day makes my heart squeeze. It was both the best and worst day of my romantic life.

I look back at Elliot and nod.

His lips thin. "Words. I like them used explicitly."

My lashes flutter. "Y-yes."

He smirks. "Do you remember that day?"

"Yes." Why does my voice sound so far away?

"Did you know I planned to kiss you?"

"N—I'd hoped."

An eyebrow tics up. "Because you wanted me to?"

The butterflies in my stomach ravage my insides, the wings flapping viciously as if to cut me if I don't tell him the truth. "Yes, Elliot. I wanted you to kiss me."

He drags his bottom lip through his teeth. "And what about now, sweetheart? Do you still want me to kiss you now?"

Yes. "You shouldn't."

"That's not the question I asked." He leans in further, letting his lips brush against mine in a whisper of a touch. My responding involuntary shiver makes him grin. "Do you want me to kiss you?"

Say it.

For once, say screw it and admit the truth, Adelina.

I try. My lips part. The breath comes to carry the sentence. But the words stick in my throat. I'm so scared of being hurt that even in times of certainty, I'm worried it's not real.

But when Elliot sighs and moves away, sense snaps into me like a harsh rubber band, and I react. My hand shoots out, gripping the front flaps of his jacket and yanking him flat against me.

Then, I smash my lips against his.

CHAPTER SEVEN

There are at least a dozen ways I hoped tonight might go, but never did I consider this possibility.

Adelina's lips are pressed against mine, and for a half of breath, I'm stunned still. Shock, admiration, and finally relief sinks through me, calming my thundering pulse. There's no more doubt or question anymore; there is only this.

A second passes, and it's all I need to collect myself and turn the tides. My hands grip the sides of her face as I angle down to take control of her mouth. She doesn't fight the exchange of power and submits, a sweet moan vibrating up her throat.

I swallow the whimper as I thread my fingers through her dark strands, pulling her closer. In the next second, I devour her whole, a multitude of things happening at once. The world stops, my heart rages against my ribcage, and my soul screams that I've at last given it what it's waited for.

Adelina was always supposed to be mine, and now she will be.

Nipping her bottom lip lightly, she immediately opens her mouth, allowing my tongue the access to dive in and taste her. Remnants of cinnamon and apple flood my tastebuds, the flavor expanding out and driving into my bloodstream. Every note is seared inside my mouth, the memory of her forever stained on my tongue.

My grasp tightens in her hair, the responding gasp she releases making my cock twitch angrily. I want more of her— all of her— *right now*. Body driven on pure desire, I walk us backward a few steps until her ass meets the edge of her desk. It's placed next to the tall window, where soft but steady snow has begun to fall. It's there I finally break free from her lips, peppering hard, greedy kisses along her jaw as my hands drop from her hair to drag along her curves.

She extends her neck, giving me the entire column to lick and bite, every touch and caress driven by her body's natural response. She arches into me, her frame melding with mine like a puzzle before it's been cut. Everything about her, about us is perfect.

Adelina's arms wrap around my neck which she uses as leverage to lift a leg and prop it at my waist. My hand finds the outside of her thigh, my fingers digging into her jean-covered flesh to anchor her to me. Even fully dressed, I can feel the heat of her core, and it pushes me further to the edge of losing what little control I have left.

I line my hips with hers, leaning away only enough to gauge her reaction when I press against her. Her head falls back, and my name is carried out on her next breath in a needy whisper.

The fabric between us is becoming even more frustrating, and I don't restrain my free hand from dipping below the hem of her thick sweater.

Her skin is soft and warm, a heavy contrast to the air circling around us. I continue to move up until I reach the edge of what feels like lace, covering her breasts.

My lips find her ear, nipping lightly at the lobe before I lick the shell. "Tell me, sweetheart. Is this how you wished that day would have gone? My cock pressed against your sweet cunt, and my hand inches away from those tight little nipples?"

Adelina's responding moan is a mixture of pure desire and desperation. If I didn't know any better, I'd say she wanted it a lot more than her words could ever admit. "Yes."

A satisfied rumble vibrates my chest, and I reward my good guess by tugging down the fabric of her bra and cupping her breast in my hand. "Has this ever been one of your dreams, Adelina? Me here with you bent over this desk?"

I feel her swallow, her breath becoming shallow as she nods her head.

I tsks, pinching her nipple hard enough to elicit a sharp hiss. "I need your words."

"Yes, Elliot. It has."

Triumph washes over me. "Have there been any others?"

She's quiet for a moment, and I pluck at her peak again while squeezing her thigh in my large palm. "Tell me, Adelina. I need to know."

"Yes," she moans, flexing her hips to push herself closer to the swollen bulge in my pants.

My blood soars as I smirk, nipping at her earlobe. "I knew you were a naughty girl. Dreaming of letting your stepbrother sink between those perfect thighs of yours. I wonder, did I ever fill you with my cum, or did you let me paint you with it?"

Her breath shudders violently, a wanton groan echoing in the space around us. I smirk to myself. It's always the quiet ones.

"I—I..." Adelina trails off, and at first, I think she's too shy to admit what she fantasizes about, but in the next second, her body tenses.

I immediately release her, backing away to see her face. Panic and self-deprivation slap me in the face as I consider if I went too much, too soon. It doesn't matter how long I've waited or how badly I want her, I should have moved slower.

"Adelina, I'm so—"

She shakes her head, onyx tendrils covering her eyes. My hand itches to move the hair away so I can see her face. Read her. But instead, she puts a hand on my chest. "We can't."

My brows pull down. "Why?"

She huffs, still refusing to look at me. "You're my *step-brother.*"

"No, I'm not. Our parents are—"

"Still together," she says before sliding off the desk and wrapping her arms around herself. "It doesn't matter if it's not for much longer."

"Adelina—" My words are cut short by the deep rumble of my father's Mustang.

Adelina jerks back as if we've been caught, her eyes widening as she quickly shuffles around the desk to look out the window. Headlights flash over the entrance as he pulls into the driveway to park, illuminating her blushed face.

My jaw hardens, my molars grinding at my dad's perfect fucking timing. *Fuck.*

"Come on." Adelina's arms tighten around herself as she reaches for the door handle, fear of being seen alone with me likely driving her feet forward. I want to reach out, to stop her and tell her that I've waited too damn long to let them ruin us yet again, but the time the words work from my throat, she opens the door and disappears down the narrow steps.

I pinch the bridge of my nose, a deep-seated bout of irritation springing roots in my gut as I follow behind her. We were so close— *I* was so close—and now the chance of telling her how I feel, how I've *always* felt, are fucking dashed. At least, for right now.

We make it back into the kitchen just as her mother opens

the front door. A swirl of dark hair flashes in front of me as Adelina hurries around the counter, scooting on one of the barstools in an attempt to appear completely normal. Despite her ruddy checks, her sweater askew, and hair that appears as if she's just run down a flight of steps, I'd say she looks only slightly aroused.

Mary and my dad enter the kitchen, both seemingly annoyed, judging by their thinned lips, but perk up the moment they see us. Dad is carrying a few bags from the store, and Mary is holding a pie box. She pushes back her oversized glasses as she beams at us.

"My baby." She holds her arms open to Adelina, who swirls in her seat, a tight smile on her face.

They embrace, and over their heads, I meet my father's eye. He shakes his head, lifting the bags, an apologetic corner of his lip curling. "Sorry we're late. The snow let up for a minute, and Mary was adamant we try to at least make it for dessert."

Mary releases Adelina, whose blush deepens when she moves to hug my father. "Of course I wanted to make it, Todd. It's Thanksgiving."

I take the pie from Mary as I wrap an arm around her, my attention planted firmly on Adelina, who continues to avoid my eye. "I can heat up the food for you."

"Such a sweet boy." Mary scoffs and leans away to pat my chest. Her dark eyes, which remind me so much of her daughter, are shimmering. "That won't be necessary. We ate at the lodge. But I would love to sit down and have some pie."

Adelina helps my dad unpack the few groceries. "Oh, Mom, I don't think I could fit another bite."

Lie. She barely put anything on her plate earlier, presumably, so we wouldn't have to sit at the table for too long.

Mary shakes her head, her short black strands whipping back and forth. "Nonsense. There's always room for dessert."

True, and I haven't had one of Adelina's apple pie cookies yet. "I'll grab the plates."

Finally, Adelina's eyes snap to mine. Her pupils are wide, her lips slightly parted as if to protest, but when I give her a quick wink, she sucks in a quiet gasp and looks away, her blush stretching down her neck.

While I absolutely hate that our parents interrupted our moment in the treehouse, I can't deny the wheels in my head that are turning, and I consider how hot it will be later when I pay her a visit. She'd be mistaken if she thought their arrival truly stopped anything. It only prolonged it.

I've waited eight years, so what's thirty more minutes?

***

Turns out a lot can happen in thirty minutes. Seated at the island, small talk ensues as Mary and my father talk about the latest week of their lives and ask us trivial things we've already discussed in the group chat. For the majority of the conversation, my eyes linger on Adelina. Her pulse quickens in her throat when she feels me staring, and she becomes more fidgety, the tension in the air thickening with each passing second. The few times she's glanced my way, I let my eyes drop to her lips, my intentions clear. And on each of those occasions, her teeth sink into her lip before she forces herself to take another small bite out of her apple pie cookies.

We play this game until her mother begins to collect the empty plates, apologizing again for missing dinner. Adelina reassures her it's fine as my father falls into his recliner and switches the TV to watch the after-game report of the football game he missed.

I put one arm around Mary, hugging her goodnight. "I actually have to be up early so I'm going to call it a night. Thank you for everything."

She nods, but a protest is clear in her extra squeeze on my shoulder. "You sure?"

"Yeah, I'm receiving an Aston I'm pretty excited about."

My father turns in his chair. "What time? I want to come by."

I laugh as I walk over and put a hand on his shoulder, giving Adelina one last glance. "Let me have a look at it before you try to put your grubby little hands on it, Dad."

He chuckles, waving me off. "Fine."

With one last goodnight to everyone, I disappear from the kitchen, up the stairs, and back into the room I called mine for almost five years.

After my high school graduation, I started working in a car repair shop downtown. I needed time and experience under my belt before I applied at the shops that worked on the cars I dreamt of. One month went by before a familiar car I'd serviced in high school pulled up. Some rich guy who drove his daddy's car like they were toys. He'd taken his car to see me at the academy after he got another ticket but found out I was now at a new place. Only now, he wasn't alone.

His rich dad found out I had been the one getting all the tickets dropped for the repairs on his son's car and asked if he could send some of his buddies' kids my way.

Three months later, I had enough money to open my own shop. But being that I wanted to build my first house, I continued living here to save up money. I was able to keep my dad company, cook and help clean up for Adelina's mom, and also look after the treehouse so it didn't succumb to the elements or neglect.

It's been three years since I've laid in my old bed and stared across the hall into the empty void of Adelina's room. The place I couldn't walk past without recalling her filling the space, her quiet hums, her cute laughter, the stacks of books and piles of paper.

It was like a ghost, haunting me with what should have been but never was.

Now, I have much darker and dirtier thoughts of what will happen in that room tonight.

I grab a towel and my small overnight bag before heading into the bathroom, moving quickly to clamber inside once the water's warm. The hot spray pelts into my back, relaxing the tense muscles with every drop. I close my eyes against the feelings as I reach for my soap, trying to focus on the calming sensation rather than the heaviness hanging between my legs.

But I can't. As I wash my body, I can't help but imagine her. Dark hair, a splatter of freckles, and thick curves I want to sink my fucking teeth into. I imagine Adelina dipping to her knees in front of me, water clinging to her hair and full lashes as she grips her tender hand around my throbbing cock.

My own hand moves down, fisting around my erection as I move at a slow and steady pace, my blood draining to my dick as I picture sweet Adelina swallowing it in her small mouth. Those perfect pouty lips circled around my length, her cheeks hollowing out as she takes me as far as she can down her throat.

A hiss pushes past my bared teeth as my free hand lifts to the top of the shower door. I grip it so hard, the metal bites into my palm, but I don't stop. I can't.

I move in time with her mouth, squeezing harder when fantasy Adelina gazes up at me from behind a row of dark lashes. She's so fucking beautiful. So perfect.

A fire erupts low in my spine, my release inching closer as I continue, harder and faster, chasing what I almost had in the treehouse. That fucking treehouse.

The place that ended it all will now be the start because now she knows.

Chapter 7

She knows and she wants exactly the same thing.

She wants me.

My blood flares as my orgasm seizes every muscle in my body, Adelina's name a tortured groan spilling from my mouth.

It could be ten fucking minutes that the electricity courses through me, frying every nerve ending, but somewhere in there, I hear it. The faint, unmistakable whimper.

My naughty girl.

CHAPTER EIGHT

How I'm able to form coherent sentences and talk to my mother right now is beyond me.

My pulse has yet to resume its normal beat, my skin feels nothing short of on fire, and the need in my core is so visceral, everything aches. I imagine it's how I'd feel at the peak of an orgasm, only to have my trusty vibrator die.

Even still, part of me relishes in the desperation lingering in my veins. It means that everything that happened wasn't another one of my dreams. It was real. Elliot and I were seconds away from finally reaching out and grasping what's been dangling just out of reach for far too long. And it was everything I thought it would be.

No—*more*. His mouth fit mine in a way that made me feel as though I'd found something that was missing up until that point. His hand roved around my body as if he'd mapped it out before and committed every curve and dip to memory. And his words. The filthy words that exposed me for the many ways I'd envision what he'd do to me.

I wanted to tell him how I hadn't just fantasized about what he'd mentioned but everything else . How turned on I was imagining pushing him to the brink. I wanted him obsessed in a way that meant I consumed his every thought.

It was dirty.

Depraved.

Taboo.

But I didn't care. I wanted to break free from the shell I locked myself in and do and feel things only he could invoke in me. But now...well, things are complicated. Our parent's arrival has altered things a bit. It's a stark reminder that at the end of the day, he and I are still technically related, and nothing should or can happen. Especially with them here.

Still, my body doesn't care about the logic behind the situation. It thrums, the nerves aching to follow behind Elliot. I'm so conflicted that I don't hear my mother until she nudges my shoulder and clears her throat.

I blink twice. "Sorry. What did you say, Mom?"

My mother sets down the rag she was using to dry the plates. She takes a step near me and lifts a soft hand, cupping my cheek. I instinctively lean into it, a small smile pulling at my lips. "I was saying that I'm sorry I wasn't always there while you were growing up."

My smile falters. "You were there plenty, Mom."

"Debatable, but Todd really helped there in the last stretch. So I was saying, even after the papers are signed next week, I hope you and him continue to speak every now and then."

My eyes flicker behind her to the stairs where Elliot disappeared. I've seen him trail up them a million times over, a small longing always playing at the edge of my thoughts as I watched him go. But tonight, it's different. My heart squeezes, confliction tearing at my chest. I shouldn't want him. I *really* shouldn't.

"Of course, Mom."

Todd waves over his shoulder. "Of course, she'll talk to me, Mary. I'm sure I'll see her plenty, too."

My gaze flashes back to my mom whose smile is knowing. She drops her hand and goes back to the dishes. "Yes, well. I ought to let you get to bed. I'm sure you'll want to head out early so you don't catch the next round of weather that's supposed to hit."

I groan, slipping out my phone to check the weather app. Sure enough, another wave of heavy snow is predicted to start after sunrise. "Okay."

I spend the next few minutes helping pick up around the kitchen before Mom finally shoos me out. I give both her and Todd a hug before finally climbing the steps.

With each lift of my foot, my pulse begins to tick erratically, my stomach invaded with the same butterflies from before. I should go straight to bed. Should pretend what happened in the treehouse didn't.

But I don't. I can't. I walk down the long hall, past my old room, only pausing to toss my phone and jacket on the bed, then take the turn and continue to the bathroom.

The door is open half an inch, allowing the soft yellow glow of the light to spill into the otherwise dark hallway. I imagine it is like the light of a lighthouse, the contrasting color calling the ships out at sea. My feet carry on without my permission, leading me to stand on the side, the small opening in my periphery.

My heart begins to hammer. If I turn my head, I'm likely to see Elliot's reflection in the mirror. See every dip and rigid muscle that was pressed against my body moments ago. It's not proper. It's an invasion of privacy.

But the steady slap of skin and water, mixed with the frustratingly intoxicating smell that makes up Elliot leaves me no fighting chance.

I press my back against the wall and let my head loll to the right, peering into the crack. Though the steam is seeping from the open door, it fogs up most of the glass, but not enough to conceal the blurred image of Elliot. One hand is above his head, gripping the shower door so hard, his knuckles are white. His head is down, seemingly focused on something in front of him.

My core tightens as I let my eyes continue their descent, stopping to watch as his chest and abs contract with a jerky movement. It's caused by the large hand he has wrapped around his thick cock, stroking back and forth.

I'm able to swallow the whimper that tries to escape my throat, but I can't stop the arousal that emerges low in my belly. The desires I had earlier come back tenfold, a vengeance I've never known coiling around me and demanding to be acknowledged. And I want to. So badly. When I reach to grab the handle, though, another thought grips me. Something dirty and likely perverse. But the hiss that escapes him only serves to yank me closer to delirium.

Without another thought, I let my own hand trail down, and my eyes drift shut. I imagine myself in the shower with him, on my knees with his cock in my mouth. I imagine the taste, the stretch, the euphoria of being there, the hard tile unforgiving to my knees, his hand unrelenting in my hair. Commanding. Taking. Giving.

My hands unfasten my jeans, and I tug them down enough that I'm able to reach the throbbing nerves of my clit. I'm so gone, so desperate, I know it won't take much...

Keeping my attention both on the mirror, and for sounds of someone creeping up the stairs, I slip my hand through my panties, my fingers dip lightly into my arousal before moving back to the place I need attention the most. Adrenaline flushing through me, I rub in hard, fast circles, my mind using Elliot's muted grunts and the pace of him fucking his fist to fuel my every stroke. I picture taking him all the way to the back of my throat, tears mixing with the water raining over him, his ocean eyes raging in a storm only for me. Only I make him this feral. Make him this desperate. Only I can make him come undone.

A tight knot forms before shooting out small currents of lightning, my orgasm seconds away from incinerating me. My nipples draw tight, Elliot's hand moves faster, and the air becomes too thin. Thoughts evaporate under the weight of the growing sensations, and when my name cuts through the door in a guttural groan, I lose what little hold I have.

My body explodes, jolt after jolt of built-up energy expelled in one swift eruption. My pussy contracts around nothing, the powerful need only growing more persistent instead of draining. So I don't stop. I keep going, prolonging my orgasm until my legs begin to shake and my knees buckle. It's only then I finally move and suck in a lung full of air.

Heart pounding against my ribcage, I fix my jeans and spare one last look in the bathroom. Elliot continues to shower as if neither of us just fell apart to the thought of the other, while I have to hold a hand to the wall to remain steady. Still, even with the adrenaline coursing through me, I manage to hurry back to my room undetected, both by him and anyone else in the house.

Disbelief and excitement wash through me as I grab a towel and one of the oversized sleep shirts I keep stored over in case of emergency. I should feel shame, but it's completely absent, in its place, desire. Desire to do it again, do more.

My heart pounds as I settle on my bed. I wait in silence, though for what I'm not sure, listening to Todd and Mom's mumbled conversation, the laughter from *Family Feud* they turn the TV to, and soon, the shower switching off.

After taking three deep breaths, I hoist myself up and force my feet to carry me back down the hall. My heart nearly folds when a towel-clad Elliot comes into view, but instead of him or I saying anything, we pass each other like two ships in the night.

Finally, a tint of embarrassment creeps up my neck as I enter the bathroom and get undressed.

What if he heard me?

No. What if he *saw* me?

It's somehow both exhilarating and nerve-wracking because I don't know the answer. If he did, was he turned on by it, or disgusted? Doubt seeps into my pores as I start the shower and step inside, not bothering to give it time to heat up. A good dose of cold water might splash some sense over me. I'm acting out of character. Doing things I've never in my life let escape the cramped cell in my mind.

I shower quickly, get out, and dry off, squeezing what water I can from my hair. When I walk back to my room, my heart falls as I realize not only is Elliot's room dark, it's empty.

Dammit. He saw. He saw and thought I was a complete perv.

A heavy sigh escapes me as I turn left into my room and slump onto the end of the bed. How could I be so crass? Why didn't I just wait—

"It's crazy how being back here feels." Elliot's sudden voice causes me to suck in a sharp breath, my hand flying to my chest in hopes of keeping my heart behind the bone.

He grins, his voice low. "You alright? I didn't mean to scare you."

I nod a little too frantically, swallowing the lump in my throat. "Yeah, I just—I thought you left."

His brows furrow as he tilts his head to the side, a still-wet clump of sandy hair falling over his forehead. "What would give you that impression?"

Shrugging, I rub my chest. "I assumed you decided to go home. You did say you had an early morning, so I thought maybe you just chose to go now instead."

Elliot pauses, his gaze narrowing. The tension in the space between us swells, the memory of everything that's happened over the past hour filling in the pockets in between. Each second ticking by only makes it thicker, the stillness so palpable it's hard to do anything else but wait.

But wait for what, I don't know.

Finally, Elliot's eyes flicker to the bed behind me. It's still the same muted green down comforter I picked out in my botanical phase. "If I ask you something, will you tell me the truth even if you don't want to?"

He totally heard me.

Heat coasts across my face, wrapping around my ears and falling down my neck. "Yes."

His gaze flashes to mine and I freeze, my heart stalling in my chest. "Back then, did you ever wish I came in here? Woke you up and took you?"

A shiver runs through me, and I force the words out. "Honestly, you could have left me asleep and I wouldn't have cared. I just wanted you."

A glimmer of something I can't read passes over him as he nods, my blush growing deeper the longer he remains silent.

Finally, he nods, a smirk playing at the edge of his lips. "And now? Would you still want me to leave you asleep?"

My bottom lip folds beneath my teeth as I whisper the answer. The confession. *"Yes."*

His gaze flits to the bed one more time before he yawns. "Goodnight, sweetheart. Don't let the bedbugs bite."

And without waiting for a response, he turns and walks into his room, but pauses at the threshold to look over his shoulder.

"Unless that's what you want. If so, just leave the door open."

Then, his door slips shut.

Elliot

CHAPTER NINE

I t takes an hour before Adelina stops tossing and turning, her grumbles of malcontent with each flip finally fading as sleep takes her. Then it takes another hour before I'm sure Mary and my father have fallen deep asleep as well. Waiting has been comparable to torture, the seconds feeling like hours as I stared at the back of my old door, counting the ridges and lines of the white-coated wood.

My heart has steadied but my mind has raced, visions of Adelina in the treehouse, ready to give me all of her if I asked, invading every thought. Her on the other side of the bathroom door, listening to me fuck myself to a fantasy of her, and the answer to my question before I left her for bed only fanning the flames.

My cock stiffens at the notion of her asleep, her body still, her beautiful face serene and content right before I slip my tongue into her tight little cunt, or push my cock past her sealed lips. So many possibilities, so many ways I could wake her with an orgasm.

It's all I thought about every single night I had to lay in this bed knowing everything I wanted was just on the other side, and tonight, I finally get to act on it.

It takes more self-control than I knew I was capable of to

wait the extra hour and a half to make sure Adelina is in REM sleep. So when the alarm on my phone dings quietly, I nearly jolt up, my cock stiffening in anticipation.

I'm careful when I open my door, twisting the handle softly before pushing it ajar. Adelina's door is wide open, her alarm clock the only source of light penetrating the dark space. The faint white color illuminates her silhouette in a soft glow, leading me into the room. I close her door and lock it, careful not to make a sound. My steps are slow and cautious, and the closer I get to the bed, the harder blood pounds through my veins.

As I approach, her soft noises reach my ear. The little hums of contentment are cute, and my dick aches to contort them into screams of pleasure.

Adelina's laying flat on her back, her dark strands fanning over her pillow, leaving her long neck exposed. The spray of freckles on her cheeks are somehow darker, the ones along her collar bone poking out beneath my oversized shirt she's wearing that's askew.

I watch for a moment as her chest rises and falls at a heavy, steady pace, her mind deep in a restful slumber. I can't help but wonder what she's dreaming about. If she's recalling events from today, or imagining something entirely new.

Naturally, she's kicked off the comforter, leaving only the thin sheet to cover her frame. It's sheer, doing nothing to hide her curves, nor the nipples poking at the fabric. The restraint I was holding on to slips, and I lift my hand, hooking a finger beneath the fabric to drag it down slowly.

Inch by inch, I expose more of her delicate flesh, holding in the groan when I reach her waist. The shirt has ridden up, leaving nothing but the small scrap of her underwear covering her cunt. The black lace acts as the pretty bow covering my present, and my hand itches to rip it off.

But I can't. Not yet. It's too early to stop my fun. I've waited too long for it—for *her*.

My molars grind together as I run my index finger along her jaw to test how light of a sleeper she is. She doesn't stir at my touch, and there's no change in her breathing pattern.

Good.

I continue to trek downward, gliding my hand down her neck, over her shoulder, and across her chest. I pause where the nipple presses out of her shirt, and circle it with the pad of my finger. Still, Adelina doesn't move, but her body responds, her nipple tightening and becoming hard. My cock swells at the sight, the reality I'll have them between my teeth soon is almost too strong to ignore.

But I force myself to continue, walking my finger across her abdomen, my pressure featherlike as I dip low to play with the hem of her underwear. Finally, a sweet groan slips from Adelina, and my eyes snap to her face.

She's still fast asleep but when her thighs squeeze together and she releases another moan, it chips away more of my control. It's true I've waited for this moment for too long, but it's the after I'm beginning to anticipate more. The moment when we come down from the high, and I can finally tell her it wasn't just her body I fucking long for, but *her*.

For that little smile she does when she's proud of a finished drawing that took her a week. The fist bump when she beats a level on one of her games. The scrunch of her eyebrows when she's so focused she doesn't notice me standing there admiring her.

Admiring all that makes up Adelina Williams.

I round the bed on her right, sitting on the edge near her waist. I place two hands on either of her knees and slowly draw them apart. I lean forward, and finally allow myself to touch her—*really* touch her—dipping my hand inside the lace.

Pulling the underwear to the side with my pinky, I slide two fingers through her slit and stifle a groan when I find she's already slightly wet.

My chest rumbles as I glide my finger up and down, playing in her slick arousal until she finally begins to stir. A free hand slides up, pressing down on her hip as I whisper, "Shh. No need to wake up, sweetheart. I'm just going to play with this wet cunt of yours. Get some rest."

She mumbles something incoherent, but keeps her eyes closed as she readjusts, opening her legs wider to grant me better access.

I smile, finally allowing one finger to sink into her. This time, I can't hold back my own groan, her heat and tight muscle wrapping around my digit making it impossible to.

She moans lazily, flexing her hips slightly.

Fuck, she feels so good. I wished we'd discussed a condom before this because all I can imagine now is her perfect cunt covering my cock, squeezing every drop I want to pump into her.

The image drives my pulse into overdrive and soon, her groggy sounds are nearly drowned from the blood whooshing in my ears. I let my thumb flick lightly over her clit as I add another finger. I drag them in and out languidly, relishing in my sleepy girl's groan and twists of her body in pleasure. She remains still, deep in sleep but she's chasing the high of euphoria.

I watch as her eyebrows furrow, her mouth parting with tiny little whimpers.

It's now I decide I'm addicted to her sounds, to the visual, and my control finally slips.

Adelina claims I've always been such a mystery, it's time she finds out exactly who I am.

A Dream

CHAPTER TEN

Adelina

At first, I'm not even sure where I am. One second I was in my condo, watching an episode of Lucifer, and the next I'm back in my childhood room, Elliot between my thighs with his fingers sunk into my pussy.

I squirm as dream Elliot drives his fingers in and out, twisting and curling to hit spots I've never had touched. It's so perfect that I can't find the energy, or even the motivation to move. I want to stay right here. Warm and cuddled, my pussy being fucked in a way that makes my entire body tremble. But the tighter my core gets, the hotter my skin is, the more I realize I may not be dreaming.

It feels too good. Too *real*.

My mind flashes back to earlier that day. The dinner, the treehouse, the shower.

The memories are hazy, erratic flashes of the events barely able to flit through my mind because of the deep pleasure drowning it out. It's all I can focus on. All I can feel.

Moans begin to slip from my mouth, one after the other until finally I force my lids to crack open. A familiar silhouette rests to my right, hazel eyes peering at me through the dark.

Elliot.

My heart and pussy squeeze in unison.

Groaning, I lift a hand to touch him, but he catches my wrist, his voice gravely and hushed. "Nuh-uh, sweetheart. Don't move. Lay there and let me make you feel good."

But our parents. I think I say it, but I can't be sure. My eyelids flutter back closed, the fear I'll wake up and find this is some sort of a lucid dream being enough to make me comply.

When he releases my hand, I let it rest over my stomach, while the other clutches the pillow beneath my head. I tilt my hips and spread my legs further, one falling off the side of the bed.

"Greedy little thing, aren't we?" Elliot's low chuckle sends a shiver down my spine. "Show me, Adelina. Show me how badly you've wanted your stepbrother to finger fuck you while you slept."

I swallow around his words, the depravity in them turning me on past what I thought possible. And Elliot feels it.

"You always tried to hide it, but now I know. This pussy is leaking for me, Adelina. It wants me to stretch it wide with my fingers before splitting it open with my cock."

A needy whimper slips past my lips. That's exactly what I want. He's all I want.

I twist my hips, consciousness pushing away the fog.

I need more.

Elliot tsks, pressing a hand down on my belly to keep me in place. "You're supposed to be asleep."

He twists his finger, dragging them out before shoving them in harder.

"Only good girls get to come, Adelina. Not naughty little sluts."

My entire body seizes at his words, the desire for both him and my release begging for my obedience. How is it possible he's making me feel so many things with only his fingers? How I'm ready to heed his every command with only a few dirty sentences?

I answer my own question in the next breath.

Because he's Elliot Rivera. The guy I knew would break my heart and so many other things if I let him.

And now, I *want* him to break every part of me, then put me back together only to do it again.

He drags his fingers out again, waiting for a few weighed seconds before thrusting back inside. My spine arches, my throbbing clit begging for the attention my G-spot is getting. If he would hit both of them at once...

"Oh, sweet girl. You are fucking drenched for me." Elliot pauses to play in the arousal that's pooling at my entrance. "Are you thinking of earlier, when you were watching me fuck my fist while you played with this sweet little cunt of yours?"

He did see.

A blush ignites my face, but I can't focus on anything else besides his barely-there touch.

It's too light—too teasing. I want to scream. To demand more from him. But I tamper my desire down, somehow sensing he wants us to finish playing this fantasy out. And so do I, because a part of me is turned on by the fact my stepbrother has snuck into my room, despite our parents being just below us.

God, I need help, but for now, I don't care.

I just want him.

Chapter 10

Elliot

Somewhere in between walking into the house and seeing her again, and her walls squeezing me like they never plan to let go, I know the wait was more than worth it.

So far, Adelina has done well at maintaining the fantasy we've both dreamt of, but now my cock physically aches to be inside her—to claim her—but not before exploring her a little more. I need to know every sensitive spot that makes her jump, arch, and groan. I have to find the places that make her needy and desperate. That makes her beg.

Maneuvering on top of her, I keep one hand working her perfect cunt, while my mouth starts back at her neck. I brush my lips over her skin softly, watching in the dim light as goosebumps pebble her flesh.

"You're so responsive, sweetheart. Are you always like this?" I move down, whispering over her collarbone. "Or only for your stepbrother?"

Her breath falters, her pussy clamping down on my fingers.

My dirty girl.

I slowly lift her oversized shirt—*my shirt*—exposing the breasts I've wanted in my mouth for almost a fucking decade. They're perfect, like the rest of her, and I waste no time trailing my tongue between the valley of them. She mewls, her upper half twisting as she tries to get her breast closer to my mouth.

I fucking love her impatience. Her need.

"Tell me, Adelina." I hover over one of her pert little nipples, lazily drawing a circle around it with my tongue. "How many times have you fucked yourself to the thought of us like this?"

The corner of her lip sucks into her mouth, but she remains still, dedicated in her obedience to stay asleep.

"You always were such a rule follower," I say, nipping at the tender flesh of her breast, and flicking my thumb over her clit. "So eager to do as you were told."

She groans louder, unable to hide her growing arousal, her growing desperation.

I fold a hand over her mouth. "Unless you want your mother to know her daughter's about to get tongue-fucked, I suggest you remain quiet. You'll have plenty of other opportunities to scream. I promise."

I continue down her frame, finally pulling my finger from her cunt. I grin when she whimpers in protest, but I'm quick to readjust, sliding between her legs.

My heart thunders, my cock straining painfully beneath me as I see the gloriously wet mess she is. So much wasted time...

I draw the lace panties to the side and take in all that my beautiful girl is. Her clit is swollen, her entrance glistening, the surrounding flesh pink from the roughness of my hand. The only thing missing is my mouth.

Both hands find a home at the dip of her hips, my fingers digging in as I press my mouth to her cunt. My first lick up her slit is slow and exploratory, the taste of her spreading over my tongue and cementing in my memory.

The sting of anger bites my spine, the reality I could have had this years ago sparking a fire in my gut.

On a level I can only describe as instinctual—no, *primal*—I don't fight the urge and turn my head to bite the inside of her soft thigh. "*Mine.*"

Adelina gasps, arching her spine before releasing a low

moan, her knees clamping around my head briefly before falling open wider.

My blood soars, my mouth returning to her entrance, where I devour her. My tongue works in angry circles around her swollen clit before dipping down, trailing around her entrance twice. Over and over, I fucking feast, my grip becoming unrelenting as I drive her to the brink.

No longer able to keep up her faux slumber, her hand reaches down, threading through my hair to push me closer, my name spilling from her in quiet gasps. The muscles in her thighs tremble as she nears release, only driving me to consume her faster. Harder.

I play with the idea of stopping altogether, allowing her the time to calm down and comply with my request before giving her what she wants. But *I* can't stop. I don't want to. I've been waiting for too damn long to see this woman come undone, and there is no amount of her disobedience that will stop me.

"Elliot, *please.* God. Right *there,*" she hisses, her fingers squeezing tighter in my hair. "I–I—"

One of her arms covers her mouth, muffling her cries of pleasure as she screams through her orgasm. I continue my assault, lapping at her cunt as if it's the last thing I'll ever eat, and don't relent until she's shaking.

When I finally sit up, she shifts her forearms over her eyes, and the other hand falls from my hair to hold her chest. Her breathing is fast and uneven, her hair tousled as though she'd yanked on it at some point, and her lips swollen as if she'd bit it.

I run a thumb below my lip, collecting her arousal on the pad before dragging slowly over hers. "Taste how good you are."

She unhooks the arm covering her face and gazes up at me through hooded lashes. Doing as told, she slips her tongue out and slides it across her lip.

"You taste incredible, don't you, pretty girl?"

She nods, her face bashful.

"Fucking delectable." Falling back on my heels, I admire the entire scene in front of me.

My beautiful Adelina's entire body is flushed, a light pink dusting over her exposed skin. Her erect nipples stab at the thin shirt that's fallen back over her ribs, while the vibrant red marks of my hand and teeth on her thigh serve as evidence of what we've done. Evidence that she belongs to me.

"You're so fucking beautiful," I murmur, running my hands down her curves. "I can't wait to see how gorgeous you are when you're stuffed with my cock."

Her lip disappears beneath her lip, desire evident in her dark eyes.

I grin, running a thumb over the bite marks decorating her thigh. I love how easy it is to stain her skin. I vaguely wonder if it will hold the branding of other things. Or will the intended design get muddled in one large pool of red?

"Time for these to go, sweetheart." I hook a finger around the lace underwear and tug hard, ripping them from her frame with a sharp snap.

She gasps lightly, her half-lidded eyes flaring momentarily as I discard the tiny scrap of fabric on the side of the bed. I'm quick to grab a condom from my wallet before coming undone from my pants. She watches me with wide eyes as I free my throbbing erection, and roll the condom on.

"Tell me you want me, Adelina." I line myself up to her entrance, nudging it teasingly as I gauge her reaction. "Tell me you want your stepbrother to fuck you."

Her pupils flare, and her answer is nothing short of a plea and command, morphed into three little words.

"I *need* you."

The hard edges of my heart soften, a foreign but long-sought-after warmth spreading over my chest. But I don't allow myself to live in it for longer than a tattered beat.

I smirk down at her, then slam inside.

Adelina

I thought I was ready for him. Thought I would be able to handle all that is Elliot Rivera.

But that was a lie.

The glimpse in the shower, the feel of him in the treehouse, even the thirty-second up-close preview as he slides the condom on didn't prepare me for this.

Elliot is buried inside me to the hilt, his hips meeting my ass, and even my forearm flying back over my face is barely enough to muffle the scream that wretches from my throat. It's been a long time, sure, but holy fuck the girth on this man.

His low chuckle penetrates the blood whooshing in my ears as I attempt to adjust to the full sensation. "Come now, naughty girl. I need your eyes on me."

My walls clench around him. Anytime he speaks, my insides quiver. I'm not sure if it's because of who we are or just my discovery that I favor his dirty words. I also like that he isn't gentle. It's not sweet and soft, but rough and possessive. Like he actually *wants me.*

But the dull ache behind my heart reminds me that this is likely it. A one-and-done to get the long-standing temptation out of our system. So I damn sure don't want to hide from him. From this.

I drop the hand covering my face, and meet his heavy gaze.

The restraint it's taking him not to move is clear in the dark storms of his irises, but they're also lined with concern.

"I know you can take it," he says, the confidence he has in me evident. But he leans closer and places a soft kiss on my nose. "But you tell me if you can't."

My teeth sink into my bottom lip and I nod, my voice nothing but a whisper. "Okay."

He gives me one last glance, but then whatever worry was there, vanishes in a hungry scowl. He pulls out to the tip, and drives inside as hard as the first time.

I silently scream, my hand flying up to grab the wooden headboard. My nails claw into the hard surface as I try to find some kind of anchor. But before I can, Elliot does it again, withdrawing and slamming back inside.

His strokes are long and hard, and stained with what feels like anger. Anger for wanting me? Having to wait? That he's attracted to his stepsister? I don't have to ponder for long because he answers the unasked question.

"I want you to feel me here for weeks. Every time you fucking move, I want the pain to remind you that I was here." His voice is more of a growl, one hand slinking up to close around the base of my neck, his thumb on my collarbone. It's dominating. Possessive. "I want the void of me to drive you fucking insane."

Again and again, his strokes hit spots I've never felt, the low pressure already building low in my belly. I turn my head, trying to hide my whimpers, the discomfort melding into pleasure so deep, tears spring to my eyes.

His hand slips up, wrapping around my neck completely so he can angle my face to him. "I want to watch you come apart for me, Adelina. I need to see that pretty face of yours when you realize it'll only ever be me that makes you feel this way."

Elliot drives into me with such purpose and force, I have no other option than to look at him. See the fire and something a little softer burning in his gaze. This is the moment where it happens. When souls fuse, and promises are whispered, but in the end, hearts are broken.

But I can't focus on that. I can't focus on anything but Elliot and the way my body is tightening all over again, the concentrated ball of electricity shooting out flares of lightning.

"That's it, sweetheart. Give me what I want." His thrusts turn relentless, and it becomes almost impossible to keep my eyes open. He feels so good. So right.

"*Now*, Adelina."

My body follows his command almost instantly, the flares of light ripping through me like wildfire. I cry out with my release that he catches with his mouth, euphoria I've never felt before coiling around my body in tight squeezes as he kisses me. It only intensifies the longer Elliot drives into me, his continued pace brutal against the same spot, causing another lash of heat to threaten to take me under.

"My greedy girl." Elliot cups his hand behind my neck to pull me up just enough to brush his lips across mine briefly. "Proof this cunt of yours was made for me."

My mind is unable to wrap around the meaning of his words before I feel them. Another orgasm slams into me violently, slicing through me with such force that darkness encroaches my vision. Elliot falters, his breath becoming ragged as his own release finds him, but he doesn't stop until both of us are panting.

Finally, his hand moves, both of them leaving my body to come up and brace on either side of my head. He levels me with a gaze I can't read, but my heart feels. It swells, both in fear that we're now over and in hopes it's not.

Whether or not he can tell, I'll never know because he bends down and kisses me until my soul splits in two.

CHAPTER ELEVEN

I 'm not sure if it's after he kisses me senseless, or when he's cleaning up my thighs despite my strong protest, but somewhere in there, he sees it. The mood shift. My body has never been lifted as high as Elliot took it, and now I'm terrified I'll never experience him again.

It's naive of me to think there is anything after this. That someone like him is the type to want to explore what could come next for us. The forbidden aspect was likely the only thing that piqued his interest, and now...

Well, now I feel as if I let my libido, and the wistful part of my heart lead me right to heartbreak's doorstep.

Still, I try to force the burn of unshed tears to ebb. It's just sex, after all. But somewhere deep down, I know it wasn't that for me. It wasn't eight years ago when I'd tried to avoid him like the plague for this very reason. It wasn't like this when I'd slowly began to peel back his many layers, storing each bit of the picture until I was able to make out the big image. And it definitely wasn't when I had to sit at dinner tables with him, work together on SAT prep, or see him in the crowd during every game I played.

This entire thing has been brewing for far longer than tonight, and I'm almost mad at myself for allowing it to happen.

Because now, how am I supposed to go on without it? Without him.

"Hey." Elliot tips my chin toward him, so I'm forced to look at him. "Where are you?"

I give him a small smile. It's forced but I hope he can't see it. "Right here."

"No, you're not." He glides the warm towel over the bite marks he left on my thigh, and I wince. It doesn't hurt as much as it is sore. "What are you thinking about?"

I drag my bottom lip through my teeth.

Be brave. *Tell him.*

My mind, or maybe the thrumming muscle in my chest, begs. I want to—I do—but I'm not that person. I don't move without weighing the pros and cons. I can't.

But when I look into Elliot's eyes and see the smallest hint of worry creasing the corners, I force it out. Even if I fall flat on my face, I can say that at least I said something.

"It's just...it kinda sucks this is for only tonight."

His brows crease. "Who said anything about this only being once?"

"You didn't plan on this being a one-time thing?"

He shakes his head, but his expression hints at the border of solemnity.

I try to huff laughter, but it comes out dry. "So what? Did you want to be my stepbrother with benefits?"

Elliot's eyes narrow. "Is that what you want?"

My lips part, but nothing comes out. My nerves tingle as if to sound the alarm, though the knot in my throat keeps me from saying anything. Maybe it's because, in reality, I'm still so unsure of him and what he wants to come from this.

So ask.

I clear my throat, swallowing hard around the lump. "What do you want, Elliot?"

He answers without a second's hesitation. "You."

The sincerity and heaviness in his words cause butterflies to take flight in my chest. They whip around in a frenzy, so lost in what to do, they make my heart pause a beat.

"That could mean so many things—"

"No." The crease between his brow deepens, and I fight the urge to reach up and smooth it. "It means I only want you. How ever you'll have me."

"So if I said I wanted to explore whatever this could be, you'd say okay?"

He's silent for a moment, his gaze drifting over my face without expression. "Would you believe me if I said I didn't need to explore what I already know?"

I roll my eyes, but inside, my chest warms. "I would say that's the effects of the euphoric bliss."

He takes the towel and stands, holding out one of his hands. "Come with me."

"What? Where?"

He juts his hand out impatiently. "Just come with me, Adelina."

Instincts have me placing my hand in his and allowing him to help me put on clothes. Once he's grabbed both of our effects, he wraps a blanket around me and leads me quietly back downstairs, where he grabs the container with my apple pie cookies. Then, he turns toward the front door.

"You want me to go outside?" I ask, surprised I didn't figure it out when he threw the blanket over my shoulders. My eyes flit toward Todd who is snoring loudly in his recliner. Doesn't look like he heard anything, thank goodness.

He continues toward the front door, sparing me a quick glance over his shoulder. "It's fifteen feet to a car I've already autostarted, meaning it's warm."

"But—" I start but stop when he levels me with a look I

haven't seen since senior year of high school when Mom asked if I had a date for Homecoming.

"Fine," I groan, bracing both myself and the thick fabric around me before shoving into the night when he opens the door.

Outside, the wind is quiet, but freezing, seeping inside everything, covering me in seconds and soaking into my bones. I shiver the entire fifteen feet, my teeth clattering comically the entire way. Elliot's long strides put him in front of me despite my speed walk, and he opens the passenger door so I can climb inside.

The moment I'm in the seat, I'm assaulted with Elliot's clean, earthy scent, the warm air eviscerating the outside as soon as he shuts the door.

My pulse thrums in my neck as I watch him stride around the hood and enter the driver's side. As long as Elliot and I lived under the same roof, we never rode together. Being seniors with our own cars, there wasn't ever a reason to. Now, I'm almost grateful I didn't have to endure it, because the temptation would have been that much worse.

The space is dark, almost intimate, courtesy of the all-black interior, and his relaxed posture with only one hand on the wheel and the other lax over the gear shift is enough to send a shiver through me.

As though he can read my thoughts, he spares me a quick glance before smirking and putting the car in drive.

We ride in silence for a few miles, and even avoiding looking over at him, my libido takes in every minute detail. The slow pace of the car, the twitch in his pinky, the three times he readjusts in his seat. Every time, my heart trips, images of him touching me invading my mind. It isn't until we turn onto the main street leading to the back of the neighborhood that I look directly at him.

"There's nothing this way. Just Old Hook's Cliff." I point out, shifting in my seat to look in the rearview.

He nods once. "I know."

My brows pull together. "I can't be outside again, Elliot. So if you're taking there to throw me off or something—"

The sound of his low chuckle sucks the air from the cabin of the car. It's such a rare and smooth sound, flowing over me and settling into the deepest corners of my soul. "I'm taking you to my house."

Confusion steals my features. "There are no houses up there. Never have been. I don't even think the land is for sale."

He grins, a cockiness to it that's hotter than it should be. "It wasn't, and there didn't used to be."

My lips part to ask more questions, but when he turns into a small strip of road, whatever question I had is answered.

Only a few meters past where the trees split, a large two-story house comes into view. Its all-black front is made entirely of slates of dark wood and iron. The only reason it's distinguishable in front of the midnight sky and haunted woods behind it is because of the lights positioned along the roof and driveway perfectly. It's breathtaking.

"This is yours? Why did no one ever mention this?"

He nods, pulling into the circle drive that runs in front of the stoned entrance. "It is. And because I asked them not too."

"It's massive. Don't you ever feel alone?"

Elliots put the car in park and shrugs. "A large section belongs to my shop, plus my own collection of cars in the garage. There are only four rooms. One is mine, another a guest room, and the others are offices."

"Why two offices?"

He smirks, but there's another emotion playing in his eyes. Something else causing him to drag his lip through his teeth. If I didn't know any better from his lack of emotional display, I'd say he was nervous. "I'll show you, but first, there's something else I need you to see."

Without another word, he exits the car, comes around, and opens my door with a hand extended. Again, I place my hand in his and hoist myself out, following him to the garage. I shiver as he unlocks it with his thumbprint on a keypad and waits the first few seconds for it to lift before he guides me inside.

The garage is massive and, like Elliot says, likely takes up a third of the bottom level of his house. The floor is slate gray, not an oil or grease stain in sight, and is home to eight cars, one of which draws my eyes almost immediately. It's the sixty-seven Impala he drove in high school, and laying eyes on it again—even for a moment—has something sticky melting over my chest. It's bittersweet seeing it again.

Still, my feet lead me toward the car, which has been shined to a beautiful mirror-like quality. My fingers reach out, trailing along the hood in a whisper of a touch, memories I thought were long forgotten springing to the forefront of my mind. I don't intend to grab the handle, but when my fingers curl around the sleek metal, Elliot's hand closes over my wrist.

"I intended to bathe you before I fucked you in the back of this car," he murmurs in the crook of my neck, his teeth grazing along the juncture.

I shiver against him despite the heat swirling in the garage. "I think a bath can wait."

Elliot smiles against my throat. "So it can."

The Reality

CHAPTER TWELVE

Elliot

Everything about Adelina was already perfect. From her sweet personality to her darkest desires, there's never been a day she hasn't amazed me. It's no surprise that after I had her, my intense interest would contort into an all-out addiction.

If she wants to take it slow and explore what's between us, fine. But after tonight, there will never be an ounce of doubt that I am hers—completely and wholly.

"Clothes. Off." My command leaves no room for debate, and to my utter fucking pleasure, she obliges.

The blanket drops first, pooling at her feet. Next, she strips from her jacket and the oversized shirt, tossing them to the side. Lastly is the pair of my sweatpants I gave her back at her mother's house. She lets the fabric fall to the floor, before stepping from them and her boots.

Completely bared, she slowly rotates, exposing her frame to me with the most beautiful blush painting her cheeks.

My heart and cock throb in unison, the visual of her so overwhelming it leaves an ache behind my sternum. I lift a hand, lightly brushing the black hair from her shoulder before trailing my knuckles down, tracing every curve.

"Stunning," I breathe, relishing the way her skin prickles beneath my touch.

Her head lolls to the side when I reach her pert nipple. "Elliot. *Please.*"

I tug on it, dragging my teeth over my lip to keep the groan trapped in my throat. "Please, what? Use your words, Adelina."

Her lashes flutter, her breath becoming unsteady. "Take me."

"Where?"

Her lips part twice, and just when I'm sure she won't say, her eyes flash to her periphery. "Here."

The corner of my mouth twitches, and I reach behind, gripping the handle of the Impala and jerking open the door. I slide in the backseat before her, then help her climb in and reposition on my lap. As soon as her naked frame sits, all patience drains from my extremities.

I grip her face and press my lips to hers. The kiss is hard and unforgiving, and as soon as I glide my tongue along the seam of hers, she opens immediately, allowing me access. I explore her mouth with no restraint, both our tongues tangling briefly. Her attempt to take control is cute, and I cut it short with a sharp nip at her lip.

She yelps softly, the movement causing her to rub against my growing erection, but she doesn't stop kissing me. Instead, she presses into me harder, her hands reaching up and tugging at my jacket. I help her by shrugging it off and throwing it from the car to join her clothes on the garage floor.

Once freed of the coat, her soft hands slip under my shirt, moving with urgency as she tries to lift it. Though annoyance flares in my gut when my lips break from hers to assist again, the arousal taking over her features when examining my chest helps compensate.

Her eyes trail over the dark marks, the black swirls of ink, and the occasional random scars. Her fingers trace over each one, a question flitting through her gaze at every new mark. I know she's storing it away to ask later because she bites down on the inside of her cheek and continues her trek south until she reaches the button to my jeans. It only takes her once to unbutton them and drag the zipper down, lifting enough to release my throbbing cock.

She licks her lips, her intention clear, and as much as I would love to feel her warm mouth close over my dick, I'd much rather watch her bounce on it until she comes apart again.

I tilt my hips up, reaching into my back pocket, and pulling out another condom. I'm quick to roll it on before sliding a hand between her thighs, and through her slit. She's soaked.

My eyes roll back as I grip either side of her hips. "Hold on tight, sweetheart."

Adelina's hands snap to my shoulders a second before I impale her with my dick.

She screams out, the new angle hitting spots much deeper than before. I give her a second to adjust while taking the moment to breathe through my barred teeth.

"*Fuck*," I hiss. "You're already dripping for me."

She tries to say something, but it comes out an incoherent mess that makes me grin. How this woman questions anything about us or my intentions is beyond me. She fits me like a fucking custom-made glove.

Once Adelina's breath isn't as ragged, I lift her hips and pull her down and back, giving her clit the perfect hit of friction. Her moans and the talon grip on my shoulders fuel me as I repeat the process, over and over. I watch, utterly transfixed as she catches the rhythm and begins to roll her hips to the pace I set. I drop one hand from her waist and thread my hand through the hair at the base of her neck, tugging her back to give me access to her breasts.

I catch one in my mouth, biting the hard peak as she sinks down on my cock again. Her head falls back, a shudder racking through her, and it's then I almost tell her. Almost say what she means to me.

But I somehow force my words to twist, deciding it's better for me to show her after this. "That's it, Adelina. Take what you need from me."

My words charge her, and soon, she loses herself. Her hips rock faster, my hand squeezes harder, and our bodies move as opposing forces, meeting in the middle with such power the car seems to inch forward. My teeth anchor into various parts of her neck and across her chest, my hand traveling the entire expanse of her body as we crash into one another again and again. Colors become muted, the windows fog and muscles begin to shake.

I'm not sure when the heat sparks, or even when her trembling starts, but it careens into us without warning and all at once.

"Elliot," she cries my name as her orgasm tears through her, sweat beading at her forehead and tumbling down her temple as she falters with the intensity of it. "*Elliot.*"

"That's it, baby." I retake control, grabbing her hips to push up to meet hers, my release barrelling into me at the same time. "Milk my cock for every last fucking drop."

Her walls clamp down, the steady release and tightening prolonging the fire blazing up my spine. My head becomes light as my energy drains, pulse after pulse of my cock twitching until finally, there's nothing left.

Our foreheads fall against one another's, and we remain connected long after our breathing settles, long after I kiss her softly everywhere my teeth indented, and long after I whisper into her skin how much I fucking adore her.

Adelina

When we finally leave the back seat of the Impala, Elliot has to hold me steady for a beat to keep my legs from buckling beneath me. He wraps the discarded blanket over my shoulders and says he needs me in the tub so I can be cleaned properly before he forces me to rest.

I silently agree, my heart still lined with worry even though it's becoming clearer that perhaps this wasn't just a get-it-out-your-system moment for him.

This was real.

For both of us.

And instead of purging our system of the long-standing tension, we opened up the floodgate.

Even still, I can't help but let the small inkling of doubt take root.

Annoyed with myself but too tired to hold an internal debate, I follow behind Elliot and into the foyer of his home. Like his car, it smells of nothing but him. It envelops me, pulling me deeper inside, even on semi-wobbly legs.

As expected, his home is modern, dark, and sleek, nothing short of what you'd see in a magazine spread of an interior decorator's ideal bachelor pad. Only when I leave the foyer and enter the living room, I'm met with a wall at least twenty feet high, made entirely of glass.

The window is seamless, floor to ceiling, and overlooks the entirety of Old Hooks's Cliff.

It's breathtakingly stunning, and for a solid minute, I'm rooted to the spot, eyes transfixed on the trees, the small waterfall plummeting into the thin creek below, and the slow trickle of snow from the low-hanging clouds. I don't even realize my mouth is ajar until Elliot saddles up beside me, tapping my chin playfully. The nervous look has returned, his eyes searching my face as he takes a deep inhale before releasing a sigh and what feels like a secret he's had for a very long time.

"When you showed me your treehouse and mentioned the wall, I thought the concept was interesting, so I incorporated it when I had this place built."

"You got an entire glass wall put in because you thought something I said once was interesting?" My eyes find his, disbelief staining my words.

One of his shoulders lifts half-heartedly. "Yeah. Well, that and after you left for college, I found myself up there pretty much anytime I wasn't working."

I'm silent as I soak in his words. It could mean so many things, and I don't want to read into it despite how hard my heart pounds in my chest.

"Even though you weren't there, I still felt connected to you. Kind of like that saying about being on two sides of the world but staring at the same moon. I don't know—it just felt right. Then, when I moved out, I knew I had to have it here."

A vicious burn radiates behind my eyes, the thick, dry knot returning in my throat. "Why?"

He turns, putting his back to the glass window to grip either side of my face. His bright eyes dance over my features, a softness I've never seen etched in every corner of his.

"Because for me, sweetheart, it's always been you. And when I didn't think I'd have you, I needed the reminder. I wanted to look out this window and remember all the things you made me feel."

Twice, I try to speak, try to articulate the way his words sink into my bloodstream and light me on fire with emotions I've only seen depicted in movies. But I can't, and luckily I don't have to. He leans closer, running his thumb over my cheek.

"I am yours. Wholly and truly. Not a day has passed since I laid eyes on you where I wasn't."

He brushes away a tear that tumbles down my face. Then he kisses me.

He kisses me in front of the window with the waterfall, in one of the offices that really is an art room he made just in case I found my way back to him, and lastly, in the clawfoot bathtub. And in between those kisses, he whispers sweet nothings, dirty promises, all of which swear that no matter what, I am his, and he is mine.

Always.

EPILOGUE

TWO YEARS LATER

A s I lay here on the hardwood table, staring at the snow falling almost too fast to discern one flake from the next, I consider my mistake.

Two years ago, I fell in love with a man who was once my crush, then turned stepbrother. He tore through my walls and snatched the heart from my chest. At the time, I was riddled with fear, with dozens of doubts clouding the majority of my decisions. But he assured me we would face them together. That he would prove what he felt for me was a once-in-a-life-time kind of love, and soon, those concerns would be a thing of the past.

And it was true.

We lasted a week before I packed up and moved into the house he built with me in the back of his mind. We made love and fucked in every room, kissed more than was necessary, and peeled back the layers of what made us who we were little by little.

I watched him work on cars. He watched me fall back into my infatuation with art. I got him into games on the Switch, and he taught me how to play chess. We hiked, camped, and discovered we liked sex in sleeping bags but not against trees.

We fell in love deeply, madly, obsessively, and just like he told me, fear and worry disintegrated. There hasn't been a day that's gone by where our souls haven't fused together a little more.

It took six months before we got married. After an only partially awkward conversation with our parents, their full support was the witness to the intimate celebration. And in the past year since, things between us have been pure bliss.

But nothing is always perfect. Nothing is without flaw. And Elliot Rivera's flaw, if you will, is that he takes everything I say and uses it against me.

Sexually. And in only the best ways.

Hence why I'm currently lying on our dining room table, naked, surrounded by candles, and mums. My cinnamon and cranberry potpourri on the stove filling the house and setting the tone for Thanksgiving dinner.

Only, instead of ham, or green bean casserole, I'm the main course, courtesy of my comment last week about wanting to be stuffed like a turkey. At first, when I caught his sly little smirk, I figured he would wake me up to his delicious cock in my mouth, or maybe fill my cunt with his cum before doing the same to my ass. But no, my beloved had much more wicked ideas in mind.

The sound of his boots hitting the tile sends a shiver over my skin, and despite the heat swirling in the air and in my core, goosebumps prickle along my flesh.

"I dare say, sweetheart, you look good enough to eat." Elliot chuckles as he nears, one hand holding a small black bag while the other threads through his tousled sandy hair. "Pun intended."

I roll my eyes playfully. "What's in the bag?"

His smile morphs into pure mischief. "Patience. I've been working all day, and I think I deserve to eat the nice, hot meal you prepared for me."

The meal he requested, and I happily and dutifully obliged. "Can I have a hint?"

"You wanted to be stuffed like a turkey, so..." Elliot's gaze heats a trail down my body, a look that never fails to leave me needy.

He drops the bag under the table before positioning himself at the head of it, sitting in his favorite spot. His hands rub up and down my calves, as he murmurs about how he's waited for me all day and thought of nothing else but sinking inside me.

By the time he grips my ankles and yanks me toward the table's edge, I'm a wanton mess.

"This first, then your surprise." He places a hand on either knee and spreads me open, baring me to him entirely.

"Elliot. So help me if there is a buttplug in that bag with turkey feathers." My voice is barely above a whisper, my mind already being hazy with preemptive euphoria.

"What if I had it custom-made?"

"*Elliot.*"

He laughs. Then he feasts.

Somewhere after I come, and then do, in fact, get stuffed in all the ways I can, I fall in love just a little more.

Acknowledgments

Thank you, my reader, for filling your time with the stories in my head.

As always, thank you to my hubs who made this book possible with wrangling the kids and cooking me yummy meals. To my kids for always walking in when I'm writing the spiciest scenes. And to my incredible alphas and betas.

M.L. Lily, Alexis and the incredible, amazing, fantastic Mackenzie

Y'all are the effing bomb and I hope you never leave me! Thank you for putting up with me being so last minute and needing everything done in one day. Like seriously. I love y'all.

Cat....GIRL! My anime BESTIE, You fucking killed this. AS ALWAYS. Thank you!

The next Holinight Novella is coming December 12th. You can pre-order it here. Did you catch the hint?

About the Author

Hey there! My name is Lee. I like to think of myself as a bibliophile who belongs to the Ravenclaw house.

I write romances that can sometimes be sweet and spicy or deadly and kinky. I'm a firm believer in happily ever afters and men who always make sure their woman is satisfied first.

When I'm not writing, I'm drowning myself in a good book, losing track of time on the Nintendo Switch with my kids, and laughing or *yelling* at one of my husband's practical jokes. (He likes to leave fake spiders and roaches around.)

Also, something important to note. I live off Chai and Dean Winchester.

Visit me on Instagram or TikTok to find out about upcoming releases and other fun things! @authorleejacquot

Also by Lee Jacquot

I wrote a couple other books!! Check them out here!

Holinight Novellas

Christmas on the Thirteenth Floor

The Four Leaf

Liberty Falls

Hollows Grove

Cupid's Peak

Mother's Day Inn

Labor Day Chronicle

Home for the Holidays

Midnight Drop

The Divine Corruption Series

Chances

Desires

Secrets

DC 4

Wicked Wonderland Duet

Queen of Madness (Book 1)

King of Ruin (Book 2)

The Emerald Falls Series

The Masks We Wear

The Masks We Break

The Masks We Burn

Made in the USA
Las Vegas, NV
19 November 2024

12156548R00062